P9-DMU-122

THE STOWAWAY

ALSO BY JAMES S. MURRAY AND DARREN WEARMOUTH

Awakened

The Brink

Obliteration

Don't Move

THE STOWAWAY

JAMES S. MURRAY

AND

DARREN WEARMOUTH

ST. MARTIN'S PRESS

NEW YORK

This is a work of fiction. All of the characters, organizations, and events portrayed in this novel are either products of the authors' imaginations or are used fictitiously.

First published in the United States by St. Martin's Press, an imprint of St. Martin's Publishing Group

www.stmartins.com

Designed by Omar Chapa

Library of Congress Cataloging-in-Publication Data

Names: Murray, James S. (James Stephen), 1976- author. | Wearmouth, Darren, author.
Title: The stowaway / James S. Murray and Darren Wearmouth.
Description: First edition. | New York : St. Martin's Press, 2021.
Identifiers: LCCN 2021016160 | ISBN 9781250263650 (hardcover) | ISBN 9781250263667 (ebook)
Subjects: LCSH: Stowaways—Fiction. | Serial murderers—Fiction. | Jurors—Fiction. | GSAFD: Suspense fiction.
Classification: LCC PS3613.U763 S76 2021 | DDC 813/.6—dc23
LC record available at https://lccn.loc.gov/2021016160

Our books may be purchased in bulk for promotional, educational, or business use. Please contact your local bookseller or the Macmillan Corporate and Premium Sales Department at 1-800-221-7945, extension 5442, or by email at MacmillanSpecialMarkets@macmillan.com.

First Edition: 2021

10 9 8 7 6 5 4 3 2 1

THE STOWAWAY

1

Most of the media had already made up their minds. They were calling Wyatt Butler the worst serial killer in decades. Depraved. Evil. A twisted, calculated madman who had preyed on innocent children. News vans and angry members of the public packed Foley Square outside the New York County Courthouse on this, the final day of jury deliberations. A heavily guarded police line held the swarm at bay.

Somewhere in the depths of the granite-faced court building, Maria Fontana approached the drab refreshment table at the end of the deliberation room, carrying a small folder. She poured herself a stale black coffee. The hum of a struggling air conditioner and a quiet ticking clock filled the room. Her eleven fellow jurors were seated around a long, rectangular table, silently sifting through the horrific evidence.

Emotional and physical exhaustion had set in long ago. Most jurors slumped in their chairs, elbows propped up on the table. Jackets off. Ties removed. Top buttons unfastened. The sense of formality from the first week had slowly but surely ebbed away. They'd been here for three weeks, deadlocked after two secret ballots. Gone through the same debates again and again. Now the judge had given everyone a final chance to reconsider before declaring a mistrial.

Maria knew that her decision would potentially send a gruesome killer to prison for the rest of his life. Or free an innocent man who had the misfortune of being assumed guilty in the court of public opinion, based purely on circumstantial evidence. Either way, the choice would be made in less than five minutes during the final ballot.

Then, I can forget all this horror . . .

The sights and sounds of the evidence she was subjected to made her stomach churn. She guessed it would take years for her nightmares to end.

Maria sipped the coffee and grimaced at the bitter taste. She would have thought that good coffee was a requirement for jury duty that took this long. She was wrong.

Guilty or not guilty. The decision, for her, boiled down to a few basic facts.

Wyatt Butler—an antique watch restorer—stood accused

of brutally murdering eight children in several different states. For sure, he was a narcissist. Maria's career as a psychologist told her that. He was outwardly self-centered and arrogant, without an apparent shred of empathy for the victims in this case. He had more than a hint of a superiority complex in the way he constantly sneered at the prosecution's claims. He was immaculately dressed in a sharp suit, lean, and clean shaven with a perfect buzz cut. His strong Brooklyn accent had filled the courtroom as he denied everything with an air of indifference, and openly mocked the police for wasting time pursuing the wrong person.

He was most definitely an asshole.

But none of this necessarily made him guilty.

The legs of a chair scraped against the polished stone floor.

Fellow juror Ashlyn Berry—who looked like Rihanna, only twenty years older—rose from the table and headed over toward the side of the room. None of the other jurors batted an eyelid as she made her way to the refreshment table.

All twelve of them had stayed in a hotel throughout the monthlong trial and deliberation to avoid outside influences. An impossible task because the proceedings were covered on every news channel around the clock. No phones. No laptops. No connection to their friends or families. And the less-than-luxurious hotel they'd chosen to house them in didn't help with the crushing boredom.

Nevertheless, over the course of the lingering month,

Maria had struck up a friendship with Ashlyn. They frequently had dinner together in the dingy hotel lobby, trying to unwind from the horrors of the case. The older juror had been overwhelmed by their task. And with the clock ticking down to the final ballot, the frown lines and nervous look had returned to Ashlyn's face.

"Which way you think it'll go?" she whispered.

"I'm not sure," Maria replied. "We each have to do what we think is right. It's hard to get past the lack of DNA and the eyewitness problems."

"I hear you," Ashlyn said. "But he sure does *look* guilty, don't he?"

Maria nodded in agreement. She set down her coffee and opened her folder. She flipped from page to page, showing the police sketches from a few of the eyewitnesses from various investigations. Each of the drawings looked different and—more importantly—none looked like the man on trial for the crime.

How could every witness describe a different suspect when the crimes were nearly identical?

It just made no sense.

That said, two pieces of evidence were particularly persuasive in connecting Wyatt Butler to the crimes. In every location of a murder, he'd stayed in the same town. On the same night. In the same chain of motels. An intrepid detective noticed the odd fact when cross-referencing motel guest lists in each city, assuming the killer traveled from town to town committing the crimes. Butler's alibi was that he was there to sell antique watches, a fact that was backed up by his buyers. But still, the odds were fairly astronomical that this was mere coincidence.

Secondly, police found a pair of freshly bloodied pants belonging to an unidentified child in Butler's attic in Bay Ridge. But the man had no children of his own, nor any explanation for where the clothes came from. The blood did not match any of the victims, so the evidence—while massively incriminating—simply wasn't bulletproof.

The decision, for Maria, rested on opinion rather than hard evidence. Yes, most in the room had already decided his guilt. In spite of this, the unpalatable fact remained. Butler had a modicum of plausible deniability.

"I just want this damned thing over," Ashlyn muttered.

"Same here."

"I wish they never selected me."

Maria rested a reassuring hand on the older woman's shoulder. "One way or another, this ends today," she said. "We'll all be home tonight. Life will return to normal, I promise you."

She gave a slight nod. "I hope you're right."

Ashlyn returned back to the table and sat down, forlorn. The case had taken a heavy toll on her spirit. On them all.

Maria took a deep breath. Thoughts about her final decision raced through her mind. Setting a potential monster free wrenched her stomach. Convicting the wrong man left the same deranged psychopath free to continue out his murder spree. Either way, her choice would leave an indelible mark on her. A constant question in her mind of which instinct was right.

She pondered her words to Ashlyn. In all likelihood, at least for her, life wouldn't return to normal, not any time soon. When she closed her eyes and thought about returning to work, only the gruesome images of the case appeared in her mind.

The gut-churning tableaus of tiny bodies, purposely configured in bizarre positions. Decapitated limbs next to torsos. Tendons stripped, cleaned, and arranged in strange patterns, giving the scenes a sinister formality. And then the weirdest part. Stretched over each of the children's corpses were oddly fitting items of kids' clothes that did not belong to the victims. A young boy wearing a yellow sundress. A four-year-old girl wearing an older boy's Communion suit.

How could Maria go back to teaching psychology at Columbia University when her own psyche was so severely damaged? How could she go home and look her children in the eye with those grisly images still swirling in her mind? Terrified that it could happen to other children, or even them?

But still, unless she was absolutely certain of Wyatt's guilt, she knew how she had to vote.

The lead juror, a portly, middle-aged man with a gray-streaked side part, stood from the table. He double-checked his watch and cleared his throat. "Guys, it's time to vote again. We all know what we have to do, and what this means." He let out a huffing breath and propped himself up by his fists on the table. "Please. Let's make this quick. We all want to get home."

The jurors exchanged apprehensive glances as they filed through to the next room. A grand, empty space with high ceilings and paintings on the wall of early-twentieth-century lawmakers and judges. It was as if they were casting their eyes down to the center of the room. Watching. There sat a booth with a curtain across its entrance. The jurors entered one by one to give their decisions on a small piece of paper. Each reappearing from behind a curtain, grim-faced.

Maria went in last.

She held the pen over the paper. Her fingers quivered slightly as she wrote her decision. She walked back out into silence, praying she'd made the right choice.

A few of the jurors appeared relieved that it was all over. At least for them.

Maria suspected that for some, the road would be much, much longer.

2

Maria left the warmth of St. James Episcopal Church, Elmhurst, back into the bitterly cold weather that had gripped New York for the last week. Her eleven-year-old twins, Chloe and Christopher, were already wrapped up in thick coats, scarves, and hats. Each edged closer to her side as she raised her umbrella. She snapped it open to cover everyone, and they headed out into the freezing rain.

Thunder rumbled overhead.

Raindrops hammered against the umbrella's canopy.

Their shoes splashed through puddles while they headed along the path toward Broadway. Only a few cars sped down the street. Unsurprising for a Sunday morning in October, with an angry sky, and the mercury due to dip again by lunchtime.

Luckily, she'd managed to find a parking space by the side of the church on Corona Avenue. Less than a minute from the church steps.

A biting wind whipped against her coat, bringing a cloud of freezing mist. The kids turned their heads into the breeze, catching the freezing-cold droplets in their mouths. Maria quickened her stride.

The churchgoers who had followed her outside audibly groaned at the inclement weather. No one had time to hang around outside and gossip.

Maria shuddered. "Step it up, guys. There's hot chocolate waiting at home."

"Is Steve making it?" Chloe asked.

"Yep."

"Last time, he put thirty marshmallows in my mug," Christopher added.

"Well, if you're lucky, he'll put thirty-one in today." Maria smiled.

The kids quickened their pace to match hers along the side-walk.

Her new boyfriend, Steve, had been great with her kids since they began dating. He was a financial advisor and part-time thespian at a local community theater, and he truly had the heart of a child. A family man for sure, but when it came to Sunday church, she knew that wasn't his jam. He broke up with God a long time ago.

In the weeks since the trial ended, meeting him was one of the only bright spots in her life. His laugh was infectious, and he never missed a moment for a well-placed joke. He was goofy, even. Playful. It had been years since she'd felt like this with a man. And though she harbored no bad feelings toward her ex-husband, he could never make her laugh the way Steve did.

He's exactly what I need.

Maria dug her hand into her coat pocket for her car keys as they crossed the intersection. When she looked back up, a woman was standing on the corner of Corona and Broadway in front of them.

Motionless.

Odd.

She was dressed in a dark coat, with no umbrella. Her soaked hair had matted against her head as if she were oblivious to the downpour. She stared at Maria and the kids as they approached. Not with curiosity. More a manic, wild-eyed expression, like she was a deer who had just spotted the silent approach of an alligator.

It wasn't unusual to encounter someone like that in this part of town. Typically high on some drug. Down on their luck. Begging. Maria had already dropped her available money in the collection plate. She peered down to avoid eye contact, sorry that she had nothing to give. Protectively pulled Chloe and Christopher closer as they crossed the street.

The safety of the car lay seconds away.

But something felt wrong.

The woman's expensive coat and shoes, for a start. The fresh makeup running down her cheeks in columns. The lines too harsh to be from the mist. And her stare—it pierced right through them.

The most unnerving thing was that the woman appeared vaguely familiar.

Maybe it was the lingering paranoia since the trial, expecting every strange look to be something personal. Then again, maybe not.

The strange woman's head turned to follow Maria and her children as they passed by on the sidewalk.

Maria quickly hit the Unlock button on her key fob. All four signal lights flashed, and the SUV let out a beep.

"Make sure you hold those kids tight," the woman muttered from behind.

Maria stopped and spun around, moving her children behind her back. "What did you say?" Maria replied.

"I used to have a boy too, just about your son's age," she said. "No more. No more . . ."

The woman's head hung low, making it difficult to make out her face up close.

"I'm . . . I'm very sorry to hear about your son," Maria replied.

"*You're . . . very . . . sorry,*" the woman replied. "You know, I don't think you're sorry at all, Ms. Fontana."

Startled, Maria racked her brain with who this woman was. "Excuse me, do I know you?"

"No. But you damn well should." The woman slowly raised her head, body trembling. Tears rolled down her face, smearing her mascara along with the spatters of rain. "I want your kids to remember my face, Maria. To know my pain . . ."

The woman moved within an arm's length. Maria instinctively pushed back, accidentally squeezing the twins backward between herself and the cold exterior of the car.

"Mom . . . ," Christopher said, clutching her arm.

"It's okay, sweetie. Let's get you guys out of the rain." Maria nervously turned to her vehicle. She opened the back door, and the kids jumped inside. "Stay inside—seat belts, please. I won't be a minute."

They nodded in reply.

She slammed the door shut and immediately locked it with the key fob. Chloe smudged her face against the glass. Christopher joined her.

For a split second, Maria tried to remember where she'd seen this woman before. She'd seen hundreds, if not thousands, of students and patients in her years as a professor and psychologist. It certainly wouldn't be the first time she'd forgotten a face from her time at Columbia.

No, it wasn't that . . .

Maria turned back toward the woman defiantly. "Who are you, and what do you want?"

Ignoring her questions, the woman continued, "Charlie turns eight next month. Would have turned eight. He wanted a new fishing rod."

Maria stared intently at the woman, still confused.

"You wanna know what *I* want, Ms. Fontana?" she continued. "I want to know if it was you."

The edge in the woman's voice had taken on a new tone. Sharper. Accusatory.

"I . . . If what was me?"

"Are you the one? Are you the one juror that voted not guilty? The one juror that caused the mistrial and set that animal free after what he did to my boy? After what he did to all those kids? I deserve to know."

Maria's head swooned with what she was hearing. Those words instantly brought back a sea of unwanted memories from the trial. Grisly images of the victims. The faces of the grief-stricken families who had the bravery to attend. The media frenzy when the mistrial was declared.

It can't be, can it?

Maria scrutinized the woman's face. It was impossible to recognize her because of her wet hair and grimace.

"I . . . I . . . ," Maria stammered, in shock at what was happening.

Churchgoers had stopped on the sidewalk, forming a small crowd around the two women. One of them, an old man named Bob, whom she only knew on polite terms, stepped in toward the confrontation. "Is everything okay here, Maria?"

"Yeah, yes. We're good," Maria said, wanting to avoid escalating the situation further. She searched her memory for a boy named Charlie.

Charlie . . . Buxton.

A seven-year-old boy who had had his arms and legs severed by the killer, and his remaining corpse dressed in a girl's pink bathing suit. The gruesome crime scene photos . . . the brutality . . .

Maria's eyes teared up as she looked at the woman. "Mrs. Buxton, I am so very sorry for your loss. You have to believe me."

Mrs. Buxton stepped closer and jabbed a finger in Maria's chest. "Tell me, are you the one who voted not guilty and set Wyatt Butler free?"

Maria drew in a deep, shuddering breath.

One of the churchgoers moved toward Mrs. Buxton to intervene, but Maria extended a hand, stopping the man in his tracks.

"I . . . I'm sorry . . . ," Maria stammered, "but you know I can't tell you that, Mrs. Buxton. We're sworn to—"

"Bullshit!" the woman exclaimed, losing her temper for the first time. "Do you know what it's like seeing photos of your murdered son every single day on the TV? Reading the description of what Wyatt Butler did to him in every newspaper?

Watching that *animal* waltz out of the courthouse without a care in the world? I deserve to know which one of you set him free!"

A shiver rocked through Maria. Her worst fears had been realized. The trial was following her. Even here. To her church in Elmhurst. The church she'd been going to since she was a little girl.

A few of the churchgoers muttered to each other. Maria eyed the rapidly growing crowd. Most of the onlookers stood stony-faced, watching this situation escalate. She couldn't blame them. She felt like she was going to faint.

Maria lowered her voice to a whisper. "I can't begin to imagine your pain, you must believe me. But . . . I'm sorry. I cannot tell you how I voted."

Mrs. Buxton's cheeks turned flush with seething anger. The sadness that seemed to encompass her moments ago had shifted. Rage swiftly took its place. She leaned in closer to Maria's ear.

"Now you listen to me," she said, whispering back at Maria. "I won't stop until I find out. The other parents won't stop. The press won't stop. If he kills again, and if I find out it was *you* that voted not guilty, so help me God . . ."

Maria didn't wait for the rest of the sentence. She abruptly turned to the car, unlocked the door, and leaped in. She slammed the lock down, pushed the Ignition button, shifted the car into drive, and gripped the steering wheel with shaking hands. She slammed on the gas. All the churchgoers surrounding the car had to practically dive out of the way.

The SUV accelerated quickly through the intersection and sped off down the street.

But deep down, Maria knew. No matter how fast she drove, she knew she would never outrun the past.

3

Maria walked briskly down Fulton Street on her way to a lunchtime meeting with her friend and former fellow juror Ashlyn Berry. The two had kept in touch, and judging by her recent cryptic text exchanges, Ashlyn was struggling with her life posttrial.

Maria had suffered the same thing too. The run-in with Charlie Buxton's mother outside the church had shaken her and her kids, and it was only getting worse. Reporters and documentary filmmakers pestered her constantly. The case still made the front page of the *Post* and *Times* on an almost daily basis. And the online abuse had grown too much to bear. Some lowlife paparazzi had managed to snap a photo of the twelve jurors leaving the courthouse and promptly posted it on the internet. Maria had long since turned off her social media, but that didn't slow things down.

In a matter of hours, a hungry team of web sleuths were able to decipher the jurors' identities. The Twitter mob relentlessly demanded to know which of them had voted not guilty. They would not stop until someone confessed. It was as if the jurors themselves were now on trial.

She crossed the street to the pedestrian area of Fulton. In the distance, the East River glistened under the fall sunshine. To her left and right, a few people sat outside the restaurants, braving the chill in thick coats.

Her phone vibrated in her jacket pocket. Maria fished it out and checked the screen.

Ashlyn messaging again, asking how long she'd be. They were supposed to meet at noon, and that was still twenty minutes away.

Someone is in a rush to see me . . .

JUST A FEW MORE MINUTES, she texted back.

Maria jogged across South Street, headed underneath the imposing concrete-and-steel structure that made up FDR Drive, and walked along the side of the river toward Industry Kitchen, one of her favorite places to eat in downtown Manhattan. A relaxing mix of the old and young, locals and tourists. A relatively safe space, she'd reassured Ashlyn.

A stream of pedestrians walked along the seaport. Joggers,

whose breaths fogged in the air. People walking dogs. None paying her the slightest attention. Exactly as she had hoped. The famed anonymity of lower Manhattan city streets had lived up to her expectations.

The maître d', a Hispanic man in his thirties, smiled as Maria approached. "Hi, do you have a reservation?"

"Yes, Maria Fontana for two. My friend has already arrived."

He checked his pad. "Yep. If you'd like to follow me."

They entered the glass-fronted building into the main restaurant. The mixed smell of cologne and sizzling food hit Maria, along with the sounds of cutlery chinking on plates and the low buzz of chatter.

The maître d' snaked between the tables to the back corner of the restaurant.

Ashlyn had sat with her back to the wall, dressed in a sharp gray trouser suit, hair plaited tightly against her head. She stared at the menu until the maître d' and Maria's footsteps approached. Then her head snapped up.

For a flickering moment, Ashlyn had fear in her eyes.

"Hey there," Maria said. "Relax, it's just me."

Ashlyn breathed a sigh of relief and stood to hug Maria. "Sorry, I've been a little jumpy lately."

"I can see that. How are you doing?" Maria asked, taking her seat.

"Had better days. No, forget that. I've had better years."

They both cracked a smile, and once they were both seated, the maître d' left the table. It was the first time they'd seen each other since the trial.

Ashlyn drew a wine bottle out of an ice bucket and poured Maria half a glass, shaking out the last few drops.

Maria's eyes glanced up to the art deco clock affixed to the restaurant wall.

11:45 a.m.

She tried to hide the hint of concern growing on her face as she turned back to Ashlyn. "You've had nearly a bottle already?"

"Can you blame me?"

"In a professional capacity, I'd tell you drinking isn't the answer," Maria said. "But, since I'm here as a friend . . ." She took a healthy gulp of wine and smiled. "So tell me what—"

"They attacked Jim."

Maria's breath caught in her chest.

"W-What? Who?"

"He works nights, you know? He came out of the Laundromat at like eleven, and there were a few people waiting at his car, demanding to know how I voted in the Wyatt Butler case. He refused to tell them, and they smashed the car windows and hit him over the head with a bottle. Over thirty stitches. It coulda been so much worse, but some folks ran outside to help."

Oh dear God, no. They finally did it. It finally happened.

Maria's heart sank. "I am so, so sorry, Ashlyn. Your husband is a good man; he didn't deserve that."

"None of us deserve this. They are coming after our families now, Maria. Our friends. How long until they come after your kids? Some of the other jurors have gotten death threats too. This isn't going to stop."

The pain in her voice and eyes was clear. She took another big mouthful of wine and rested her head in her hands. "I just want this over. It's killing my family. It's killing me. Everywhere I look, it's like people know. I'm the one being judged."

The jury hadn't broken silence since the trial. Everyone had agreed to that as a collective responsibility, mainly to stop the blowback against whomever had chosen to find Wyatt Butler not guilty. But clearly, their plan had backfired. Their silence was only making the public outcries more insatiable.

How long until one of us gets seriously hurt . . . or worse?

"I'm not sure how much more of this I can take," Ashlyn said, wiping away tears from her cheek.

Maria lowered her head, lost in thought. The entire jury was living through a new hell. This torture would continue until one of them spoke out, until one of them accepted responsibility and admitted what they had done.

Maria cleared her throat. Took Ashlyn by the hands. "Listen to me, okay? You're my friend, and I want you to know you're not alone. We're gonna get through this together."

Ashlyn nodded as the tears freely streamed down her face.

"And I want you to know," Maria continued with a newfound resolution in her voice, "that by this time tomorrow, all this will be over. You have my word."

Reporters packed inside the Columbia University's Cowin Center auditorium. A few of them fumbled with the swiveled desks attached to each of the lecture hall seats, trying to prop up their laptops and notepads before the main event started. Maria stood out of view, in a doorway to the left of the stage. She'd arranged this press conference in less than twenty-four hours, with the university's approval. The consequent interest had been off the charts.

Butterflies fluttered in her stomach.

Her boyfriend, Steve, had reluctantly agreed to her plan, despite his deep reservations and after an almost sleepless night of cautious discussion. He towered by her side in his business suit. Hand on her shoulder. Grim smile of resignation across his bearded face. Regardless of whether he wholeheartedly agreed with her decision, she still appreciated the support.

The lights on the auditorium's stage brightened.

The entire area fell silent.

Hundreds of journalists sat with notebooks in hand. Voice recorders raised. At the back of the room, red lights burst to life on TV cameras.

She checked her watch. Exactly 11:00 a.m. She had made good on her promise to Ashlyn.

Maria brushed her hands against the fabric of her beige pencil skirt and climbed the stairs, trying her best to appear relaxed. As a senior lecturer, she'd given hundreds, if not thousands, of speeches in rooms just like this. But nothing felt quite the same. Nothing had the potential to destroy her like this.

She moved to the central lectern and the phalanx of microphones that had been positioned to its front. She placed down a sheet of paper containing bullet points.

The lights onstage shrouded the audience in darkness. Figures sat stationary, waiting for their scoop. And they'd get one.

So would the millions of eyes that were watching too.

Here goes nothing.

She took a deep breath and faced the cameras. "Good morning, ladies and gentlemen. First, thank you for coming today. I'm here to make a short statement and will take no questions."

Maria glanced across to Steve. He gave her a reassuring nod.

She swallowed to placate her dry throat and continued, "My name is Maria Fontana, and I am the head of the Psychology Department here at Columbia University. I was also one of the twelve jurors in the Wyatt Butler trial."

The crowd murmured restlessly.

"To begin, I'd like to say my heart goes out to every victim, their families, and friends who have suffered through these heinous crimes. No one in the world deserves to go through such a thing, and as a mother of two, I cannot begin to imagine your grief. My heart breaks for you, and please know my prayers, and so many of our prayers, are with you always."

She paused for a long moment to let her opening words sink in.

"Secondly, over the past few weeks since the trial ended, my fellow jurors and I have received terrible abuse from the press and the public. Everything from physical confrontations in the streets and at our places of work to outright death threats against us and our families. This cannot be."

Total silence consumed the room. Each set of ears hung on her every word.

"Whether you agree with the outcome of the trial or not, I can assure you my fellow eleven jury members were all fair-minded people with a desire to come to the right decision. A decision made in the privacy and anonymity of the deliberation room, as per our constitutional right, based on the facts presented to us in a fair and impartial way. We naively thought it would be possible to simply return to our lives once the trial ended. But I see now that this is not possible. That this will not end with our silence."

Maria grabbed a glass of water and took two greedy gulps. Mentally composed herself for the words she was about to say.

Dear God . . .

Please let this be the right thing.

Please.

It has to be.

She grabbed both sides of the lectern with her hands and continued, "So, for the well-being of my fellow jurors and the safety of all our families, I am here today to tell you that *I* am the juror who voted not guilty in the case."

A few in the crowd took in sharp breaths. Bright flashes from high-end cameras burst throughout the room. The sound of shutters crackled at lightning speed. Maria spoke up, intent on being heard above all the clamor.

"I take full responsibility for the Wyatt Butler mistrial. In all good conscience, I couldn't convict a man based purely on what I believed to be circumstantial evidence, no matter how strong it appeared. If even the slightest reasonable doubt exists, and that's all it has to be, then I felt I had no choice but to find Wyatt Butler not guilty."

Condemnation and commotion spread throughout the lecture hall as reporters frantically took notes. The tsunami of voices struck Maria like a wall of sound. Some yelling questions. Some yelling obscenities.

She guessed the same reactions had been repeated around the country.

Maybe the world.

For the next few days, or weeks, or months, she knew she'd be the bull's-eye for the press and public's scorn. But there was no other way to protect her fellow jurors.

It's the right thing to do . . . the only thing I can do.

A bead of sweat trickled down her back.

Her legs trembled, but she had to see this through with a veneer of confidence.

Maria gripped the lectern harder and leaned in closer toward the microphone, signaling to the audience to quiet down. "I'd like to finish by pleading with everyone to respect the jury's privacy. Refrain from attacking them. Support the people who had to make the hardest decision of their lives and have to personally live with the consequences each and every day. Thank you."

With that, Maria spun away from the lectern and headed to the side of the stage, her body shaking from nerves.

Another torrent of questions erupted from the audience.

She ignored them and focused ahead. Steve dutifully held his arms open, ready to embrace her. All she wanted to do was rush to the restroom and vomit.

Maria grabbed him by the hand and dragged him past the staff. She thanked them and hurried along the hallway.

Steve strode level with her. "I'm really proud of you, love."

Maria felt an old sensation. Something she hadn't experienced in a long time. The feeling of wanting to burst into tears. But what good would it do? Nothing would undo what had just happened in there. Nothing would bring life back to the way it was before the trial.

"I just hope it's enough," she replied, not quite believing her own words.

4

EIGHT MONTHS LATER . . .

At nine in the evening, Maria parked her car in the driveway of her 1930s-style Elmhurst house. The last day of the fall semester had been completed, and with that, a chance for a few weeks at home. Away from the constant questions. The lingering stares. Conversations with her colleagues that were crudely loaded with subtext.

Light glowed from a crack in the living room drapes. The kids would be in bed, but Steve typically had a bottle of wine ready and a movie already selected on Netflix.

All she wanted to do was put her feet up and relax with the love of her life.

Spending time at home with her kids and Steve was her

safe haven. Had been ever since the press conference eight months ago.

Maria slung her laptop bag over her shoulder and headed through the cool night air to the front door. Twisted her key and entered into the welcoming warmth.

"Steve, I'm home," she called.

"In the kitchen, love."

The original floorboards creaked under her shoes as she headed through the hallway. Steve sat at the head of the table in their farmhouse kitchen. He was still wearing his Shakespearean costume from his dress rehearsal—a wool tunic with a tartan sash. And he'd already downed half a bottle of pinot grigio.

He gazed up at her. Straight-faced. Blurry-eyed. "Good evening, fair maiden."

"Hello, my sweet prince," she replied, leaning in to give him a kiss. "Everything okay?"

Steve frowned in response. "We got another one of those damned packages." He pushed a thick brown envelope toward her. "But this one is different. I think you should take a look."

For the last few months, she'd received a steady stream of mail about the court case. Mainly a mix of nasty letters and others from twisted people who were obsessed with the trial, desperate to know more. And still, on occasion, the odd death threat would arrive, which she would promptly hand over to the police. Steve had always acted as a filter for the correspondences, making quick work of shredding the letters and tossing out any strange objects sent their way. But this was the first time he'd asked her to look before giving her a brief description.

He pushed a glass of wine toward her. "Have a drink first."

"Like that'll help."

Maria wrestled off her coat and sat on a chair next to him. She analyzed the bulky envelope.

"There's no return address," she said.

"No shipping label either."

Jesus.

"Which means someone left this in our mailbox." Maria sighed. "It's one thing to send us mail. But when these fanatics start showing up at our home, that's where I draw the line, Steve."

The thought of it made her twist with anger.

How dare they.

How dare they think they have the right to come to my house*!*

She felt the indignation growing inside her. Maybe Steve was right. A drink might be just what she needed. Maria reached over and stole a swig from his wineglass before drawing the bulky envelope toward her, debating whether to pull out the contents.

"All right, let's see what this asshole wants."

Maria reached in and slid out a brand-new hardcover book.

Wyatt Butler: The Ultimate Truth by Jeremy Finch.

"Oh God," she whispered to herself.

She recognized the name immediately. This writer—Jeremy Finch—had pestered Maria for an interview nearly a dozen times. After every occasion she had turned him down, he had gotten more and more aggressive, even threatening to expose her private conversations in the deliberation room. She'd assumed he was bluffing. She'd also assumed that no reputable publisher would consider his amateur-sleuth conspiracy theory trash. His online blog contained plenty of poorly conceived conjecture and little substance.

But here it was—a self-described tell-all book.

Stamped with the logo of one of the biggest publishing companies in America.

Maria flipped open the cover.

The inside of the jacket had a picture of Finch's smug oval face. Circular glasses. Immaculately trimmed goatee. Wearing a scarf indoors. Chin resting on his fist in mock contemplation. A walking cliché that had somehow found an editor happy to make a fast buck off the back of his bullshit.

"I think you should read it," Steve said.

"Why? What's the point?"

"I've seen tons of posts in the forums and on social media. Plenty of folks believe what this guy writes, whether it's true or not. Might help to at least know what people will be saying, what you might have to deal with moving forward."

She scowled at him. “I told you to stay away from those message boards about the trial. You're always on them, Steve.”

“I lurk for your sake. That's all.” Steve stole the glass back and took a big slug of wine. “Check out the next page.”

Maria flipped the page and gazed down at a handwritten inscription below the book title, three words in total: ***You. Were. Wrong.***

Her face flushed with anger. “This son of a bitch. He's taunting me.”

“You think it was Finch that left the book for you?”

“Do you even need to ask?” Maria unlocked her iPhone and looked up the title. “It says here the book comes out in stores tomorrow. This is an advance reader copy. It's Finch, all right.”

The temptation to skim-read was huge, just to see how wildly inaccurate and ridiculous the book was. And no doubt he would sell a million copies, being the first book about the trial to come to market. That's undoubtedly how he got the publishing deal in the first place.

Maria folded the next page over and scanned the table of contents. One line immediately caught her eye.

Chapter 16: Maria Fontana

Her jaw clenched.

That son of a bitch.

“How can he write a chapter about me when he knows nothing about me?” she exclaimed.

Anger got the better of her. She yanked the wineglass back over, took a swig, and fanned the pages to the section dedicated to her.

It was pure libel. Every word of it. Essentially, a fiction he fabricated based on total conjecture. He'd presented Maria as a struggling academic with a failed family life, claiming wildly that her own guilt over a previous broken marriage had led her to find Wyatt Butler not guilty.

"This is complete bullshit!" Maria shouted. "The 'connections' Finch is making are beyond ridiculous. They're insulting! Anyone with half a brain can see that."

The character assassination continued. Page after page of total garbage.

Supposed quotes from Maria's former students, saying she fell apart when her first marriage broke up. Other sources saying that she would not listen to reason in the jury room, and always planned on voting not guilty, facts be damned.

Of course, every *source* was nameless.

There was even one portion speculating that Maria had intentionally set Butler free in order to skyrocket herself to fame. It continued that her plan was to use her newfound celebrity to transition into becoming a TV personality, an on-camera psychologist with her own talk show examining the worst serial killers in history.

The entire idea was preposterous.

Maria turned to the last page of her chapter.

Steve reached over and grabbed her free hand, giving it a tight, comforting squeeze.

Finch had claimed that Maria acted like a coward in the face of overwhelming evidence. And for this, he wondered how she could live with herself. He manipulated all the circumstantial evidence to make Wyatt Butler appear like the most open-and-shut case since John Wayne Gacy. And to make her look like a fool and a quack.

Maria snapped the book closed and shoved it across the table in anger. "This lying bastard."

"I know, love," Steve replied, squeezing her hand.

"He's perfectly content ruining my life for the sake of selling a goddamned book."

"Let's fight back, then. One of the guys at the theater is a pretty damn good lawyer. Let's give him a call, see if he can—"

"I've got one better," Maria interrupted, looking at her phone. "It says here Finch is autographing copies of the book tomorrow at the Barnes & Noble in Union Square. Let's go pay this asshole a visit."

Steve slumped in his chair and shook his head. "Now how did I know you were gonna say that?"

5

Maria glared at the *Meet the Author* live appearance photo hanging in the Barnes & Noble store window. Seeing Finch's face blown up to this size made him look like an even bigger jerk. A larger-than-life loser. She dreaded seeing him in person, hearing the lies he would undoubtedly be spewing to the crowd.

Even more, she dreaded hearing the gruesome details of the case she was so much trying to forget. It was almost as if Finch wouldn't allow her to ever move on, and he was definitely keeping the trial fresh in the public's mind.

Maria and Steve entered the welcoming warmth of the store. As Steve instinctively removed his hat and scarf, Maria kept hers on. Not wanting to risk the chance of being recognized. Not until she could tell Finch off, face-to-face.

People stood around the shelves, scanning the book spines or reading blurbs. Nobody gave Steve or her a second look as they headed toward the escalator at a fast walk.

She nervously grabbed his hand as they ascended toward the lecture space. When they reached the top floor, a decently sized crowd had assembled in rows of chairs. Maybe several hundred, with only a few spaces available.

A youthful-looking store rep stood at the podium, mid-introduction.

Maria and Steve quietly found two seats near the back.

"—from his extremely popular blog, and now, soon-to-be-bestselling book where he dives into the untold truths of the Wyatt Butler case. Ladies and gentlemen, please welcome Jeremy Finch."

The audience applauded enthusiastically.

Maria's stomach knotted.

Finch stepped out from behind a large bookshelf, dressed in a tweed jacket with elbow patches, a pair of extraordinarily pleated pants, and his signature ascot.

To her, he looked like a jackass.

Seeing him in person made her feel sick. He was even shorter than she'd imagined in her cruelest of caricatures.

"Someone is trying *real* hard to look like an author," Steve whispered to Maria.

"You're telling me."

"He looks like the 1970s wrote a book," Steve continued, making Maria stifle a laugh. She pinched him on the arm.

Finch approached the podium with a smug grin plastered across his face. He mouthed *thank you* to the audience several times. Then he jogged up the steps. Leaned in too close to the microphone. "Good afternoon, everyone. My name is—"

A high-pitched feedback loop screeched through the speakers, and the representative from Barnes & Noble gestured for Finch to lean back a bit from the mic.

Jackass, indeed.

Maria tried to compress the chuckle building at the back of her throat. *Even the microphone doesn't want to hear what he has to say.*

"Sorry . . . um . . . excuse me," he continued, sweating. "My name is Jeremy Finch, and I am the man who wrote the . . . I mean, I am the author of *Wyatt Butler: The Ultimate Truth*. So . . . my book delves into the untold details of the most heinous serial killer of the past fifty years, details I've assembled through painstaking research, and unprecedented access."

Steve squeezed Maria's hand. She was trying her best to remain calm but could feel the anger welling up inside at her unfair and dishonest portrayal in the book.

Finch continued, still sounding like he was taking a final exam in his high school public-speaking class.

"—hundreds of hours' worth of interviews with detectives,

witnesses, and the victims' families. By the end of my book, you will be shocked to learn the entire truth about Wyatt Butler, and be more furious than ever that this killer was acquitted because of one troubled juror, and is now back out there, on the loose. So watch your kids closely, because—"

Maria bolted upright in rage, startling the audience members seated around her and Steve. "You lying son of a bitch!" she shouted.

The crowd quickly turned to see where the commotion was coming from, zeroing in on Maria. Steve jumped up, trying to calm her down, to no avail. Clearly, this is not how he'd imagined she would confront her tormentor.

"How dare you!" Maria yelled. "You were not there, you don't know shit about me or anyone else on that jury. We did our job and voted based on logic and evidence."

The crowd murmured in realization as to who she was. Several folks quickly pulled out their cell phones and began to record the tense scene unfolding in front of them. The store manager called on a radio for security to come to the top floor.

Maria held up her copy of the book, continuing, "This piece of shit isn't worth the paper it's written on."

Finch's face turned from startled to bemused. "Wow, hello there, Ms. Fontana. You might recognize Maria Fontana from chapter 16 of my book, everyone. She's the one who recklessly set the killer free."

"Go to hell!" Maria shouted back. "And if you ever come to my house or write this shit to me again, I'm calling the police."

With that, Maria threw the book onto the floor next to the podium. It crashed to the ground faceup, with the inscription page open toward Finch. Two security guards rapidly approached from the nearby escalator.

Steve nudged her by the arm in a "it's time to go" motion. She obliged before security forcibly threw her out, and they headed toward the exit willingly.

At the podium, Finch leaned down to pick up the book on the floor and read the inscription.

"*You were wrong*," Finch read into the microphone, calling to Maria as she stepped onto the down escalator. "Ms. Fontana, while I agree wholeheartedly with the sentiment, I'm afraid I cannot take credit for writing this, or for ever visiting your home. I guess you must have a secret admirer."

Maria jabbed up her middle finger directly at Jeremy Finch as she stepped out of view.

She knew how she must've looked. How much her outburst likely played right into Finch's hands. Fitting his description of her perfectly.

But she didn't care.

She wasn't going to sit there and take it quietly. Her reputation was on the line. And if she wasn't going to defend it, who would?

The tears she had so desperately shoved down after the

conference all those months ago—the tears she'd been fighting practically since the trial—came out in a torrent of furious sobs.

As they descended the escalator, rage still burning inside Maria, Steve turned back toward her and whispered, "I promise you this. He'll never, ever hurt you or our family again."

6

Maria sat on the opposite side of the desk to Professor Liander, one of the deans at Columbia University. Behind him, sunlight seeped through the cracks in the blinds, highlighting dust motes in his oversize office.

Certificates and awards adorned the walls, some yellowed from age.

But Liander wasn't admiring his own accomplishments. He stared pensively at his desktop monitor, stroking his salt-and-pepper beard.

Maria winced at the sound of her own voice through the speakers.

And again at the sharp intakes of breath on the YouTube

clip when she flipped off Jeremy Finch and stormed out of the bookstore.

Liander shuffled his mouse across its pad, clicked, and watched the clip again. He slowly shook his head and let out a deep sigh. Like a disappointed parent when he'd read a terrible school report card.

Last time Maria had checked, more than three million people had watched her confrontation with Jeremy Finch. Certainly more than enough to earn the title of "viral."

The clip ended a moment after one of the staff breathed, "Oh my God."

Liander swung in his chair to face her. "Maria, I want you to know I'm on your side. I can't imagine what you've gone through the past few months, how your life has been upended. But this . . ."

Maria knew where the conversation was heading.

Liander said, "I can defend you against false accusations. I can defend you against unwarranted attacks. But I can't defend the head of Columbia's Psychology Department going to a bookstore to confront some hack, only making matters worse. You've turned this Jeremy Finch character into a goddamned *New York Times* bestselling author overnight."

"Yes, I realize that. I'm sorry I let my emotions in the moment get the better of me."

"It's understandable, truly, but you know how this looks for the university."

"I do, and I'm prepared to follow your lead."

Liander offered her a thin smile. "So, here's how we proceed. I need you to take a mandatory leave of absence. We can call it a sabbatical, which you're eligible for regardless. Take the year to work on a research project, spend more time with your family, go on vacation. Hell—all three of those things. Whatever you'd like."

Maria sat forward. "A full year?"

"As long as it takes for this to blow over. And in that time, I need your word that you'll stay out of the spotlight."

"So in simple terms: vanish until you're no longer a liability or we'll fire you?"

Liander's features softened. "Columbia is your home, Maria. I want you back in the department. You're one of my best. Take some time, and then come back to where you belong."

A year sabbatical . . .

A year would feel like an entire lifetime to her.

But she understood why this needed to be done.

"Okay. I will."

Liander smiled, visibly pleased with Maria's choice. "Good. I'm glad you agree. And while you're gone, I'll have Professor Zharov take over your responsibilities as head of the department."

Maria couldn't believe her ears.

Zharov?

A low-level adjunct who'd barely been cited in any of the major psych journals?

Liander gave her a wry smile.

"Kidding. Your job will be waiting for you when you come back."

Maria laughed, instantly grateful for the bit of levity. Liander grinned and reassured her.

"Remember, I'll only be a call away if you need anything."

"Likewise. I'll stay in touch."

"I expect you to. Give those kids a hug for me."

The two shared a bittersweet smile. Liander rose from his chair and offered his extended palm.

Maria shook his hand. "Thank you, Dean. I'll see myself out."

She turned and headed out of the office into a brightly lit corridor toward the exit. She looked up toward the sunken ceiling above, soaking in every step as she walked out of the hallowed halls that had become her second home. Maria breathed in the musty old-book smell that had always scourged Schermerhorn Hall—the smell she had initially found repelling during her first few years. But had since grown to love.

Sure, she'd be away from her job a lot longer than expected, but the best way to deal with this was to come at it with positivity.

Quality time with the kids and Steve. A clean break, away from the renewed Wyatt Butler hysteria.

Away from the negative forces that would only continue to haunt her if she stayed in the public eye.

Maybe this time off would be a good thing.

7

TEN MONTHS LATER . . .

At two hundred thousand tons, HMS *Atlantia* was a behemoth. The bright white steel of the hull glinted in the late-morning sunlight and reflected off the Hudson, sending shimmering beams up toward the gangway. It was one of only two cruise ships in the world that regularly made the long transatlantic voyage between New York and Southampton, and Maria felt extra lucky that Steve snagged tickets when he did. Since they would be married in two months, the cruise kind of felt like a pre-wedding honeymoon.

It had been a year of firsts. Steve's first big promotion. Chloe's first crush. Christopher's first football game. And Maria had been there for all of it. For that, she was grateful. But on the other hand, the lack of coursework to be graded and curriculums to prepare left her with loads of free time. Maybe too much free time. Dean Liander even made her pass off the bulk of her patients to another colleague in the department.

A quote her mother always used to say had swirled in Maria's ears for months.

An idle mind is the devil's workshop.

She'd picked up some new hobbies here and there. But all those days spent at home alone had started to wear on her. There was only so much gardening, calligraphy, and jewelry-making one woman could do before the monotony began to wear on her again.

This cruise couldn't have come at a better time.

It would be Chloe and Christopher's first trip to a foreign country. Maria figured the UK in the summertime would be perfect. Safe. Nice weather. Nothing too crazy. Maria was just about to click purchase on the flights when Steve proposed a better idea.

By the time her family arrived at the cruise port, the majority of passengers had already gone through. As a result, they'd breezed through the check-in process at the terminal. The kids' newly minted passports were cleared, their bags were scanned and loaded up onto a cart, and now, they sauntered down the gangway toward their home for the next twelve days.

We were smart to arrive later.

As much as Maria was excited to travel, she was still nervous to be on an enclosed ship. All it took was one person to recognize her. One person to cause a scene, and then she'd be ostracized the entire voyage. She prayed the news cycle in England was a bit more forgiving.

The kids played hopscotch behind the porter's cart. Stacked sets of suitcases rolled over each panel of the gangway with a heavy thud.

The moment they stepped foot onto the ship's promenade, the twins took off running.

"Hey, get back here!" Maria called after them.

"It's okay. Let 'em explore," Steve nudged. "Where are they gonna go, anyways?"

They headed along the deck in the same direction, eventually catching up with the kids near the shuffleboard court.

Maria glanced over her shoulder back toward the gangway. She squinted through the glass windows of the movable bridge. No one inside. No other passengers had made their way behind them, either.

Wow. We really might be the last people boarding the ship.

Three soft bell chimes rang out through the ship's PA system. A woman's voice, somehow gentler than the bell, filled their ears.

"Hello, passengers! It's a beautiful day here in New York Harbor. At this time, we ask that you please make your way to the pool area on Deck 13 for our onboarding orientation and safety review. Welcome aboard the HMS Atlantia*!"*

Maria and Steve located a deck plan posted near the elevator bay, collected the rambunctious twins, and made their way up to the pool area.

The lido deck was a magnificent sight. Two massive crystalline Tahitian pools sparkled beneath the clear sunshine. Rows of hot tubs lined each end of the deck, saddled up beside a coffee shop, four different bars, and another smaller kiddie pool.

Passengers had packed around the larger of the two main pools. Hundreds of them. Sweaty elbows brushed up against one another. The smell of body odor already hung strongly in the air. But Maria didn't mind. In a way, it felt good to be around people who didn't recognize or accost her.

Here, I'm just another face in the crowd.

The orientation was brief but informative. Maria listened closely and took notes in her pocket journal while the head of guest services breezed through lifeboat procedures, safety checkpoints, and emergency protocols. Chloe and Christopher rolled their eyes the entire time.

The presentation ended in a ship-wide round of applause. Passengers dispersed in a mass exodus, heading off to unpack their clothes or explore the various amenities the ship had to offer. Lanyards swung from happy necks. A large portion of the herd beelined straight for the all-you-can-eat buffet.

Maria wrapped her arms around her children. "All right,

guys, let's head to the room to get settled." She ushered the excited twins back toward the elevator.

"Whoa, whoa, whoa." Steve stepped in front of them. "Not so fast, guys. You wanna waste all this sunshine in a cabin? No way!"

"But our luggage is waiting for us—"

"Oh, don't worry about that. The bags will be fine. The porters already took care of it for us. We can do all that boring stuff later."

He glanced across the deck in the direction of the bar. "You stay here. I'll go grab us some drinks."

"What? Now?" Maria smiled. "Isn't it a little early to be drinking?"

Steve looked back at her with a coy smile. "Don't make me say it. It's already five o'clock in England, baby! I'm on London time!"

Maria threw her head back and laughed. Steve leaned down and planted a quick kiss just above her hairline.

"I'll be right back. You stay here and soak up some rays." Steve headed off, then glanced over his shoulder. "If I come back and you guys are tanner than I am, you're all in big trouble!"

"We're *already* tanner than you!" Christopher teased.

Walking backward, Steve mimed holding up one of those old tanning reflecting boards.

Maria playfully nudged her daughter. "Oh, I can't wait to

see him burned like a lobster in a few days!" With a last name like Brannagan, there was no way Steve would tan better than she would.

She absentmindedly ran her thumb over her ring finger, feeling the newest addition to her wardrobe: a platinum engagement ring. The single solitary diamond gleamed in a prism of colors beneath the sunlight. She had known Steve was going to propose eventually, but she hadn't expected it to happen so soon. But when he asked during a casual dinner at home a few weeks ago, it felt right. She even surprised herself with how quickly she'd said yes.

"Mom, can we go check out the waterslide?" Christopher pleaded.

"The waterslide? I don't think it's running yet, sweetheart."

"I just wanna go look at it. We promise we won't do anything."

Maria glanced around the pool deck. It had cleared out pretty quickly. Only a few families remained. None using the yellow slide at the far end that coiled into the water. The twins looked up at their mother with puppy-dog eyes. Since the trial, she'd kept them both on such short leashes. Maybe this was the time to loosen the grip.

Let them have fun.

"Please, Mom," Chloe pressed.

"Okay, but stay where I can see you. And stick together."

Huge grins spread across both of the kids' faces.

"Thank you!" Christopher replied. "We'll come straight back."

Maria watched as the twins skipped away. She followed them closely until they reached the slide, each slapping their hands against the banana-colored PVC siding. Within a second, they'd both kicked off their shoes and were clambering their way up the stairs.

That twin telepathy. I should've known.

Her son shot down first, zipping down the slide and crashing into the water.

She felt a smile extend into her cheeks. *Great. Wet clothes on day one.*

She watched as Chloe followed her big brother's lead. Big brother by only two minutes, if you asked her.

Maria slowly exhaled and peered up. The sun blazed down in the clear, baby-blue sky.

Now she could relax.

In her peripheral vision, a thin, white wisp sailed through the air. A seagull, leisurely gliding on the eastern breeze. Maria watched as the bird descended toward the ship. Probably hoping to find a forgotten tray of french fries or some crumbs to pick at. It landed on the upper-deck railing and stretched out its black-tipped wings.

Maria's heart caught in her chest.

A few feet from where the gull landed, a man stood leaning against the rail.

Alone.

Peering down at the pool area.

Searching, yet with no urgency.

His bulky knit sweater and heavy cargo pants made her frown. They were far too warm for the heat of a New York summer. An old worn hat cast a deep shadow across his eyes.

But it wasn't just his attire.

Something about him seemed . . . off.

He was out of place.

The man's head turned slowly toward Maria. His listless stare resting directly upon her own gaze.

Their eyes locked for a split second.

A shiver shot up Maria's spine.

"Your margarita, my darling!" Steve burst in, spilling some of the beverage out from the side of the glass as he extended it toward Maria. "I asked if they could swap out the salt on the rim for sugar like you like it, but the bartender just laughed at me."

Maria returned her focus back to the railing.

But the man had gone.

"You okay? What is it, baby?" Steve asked.

She scanned along the rail. The walkways. The surrounding pool furniture. Nothing.

"Baby? What is it? What'd you see?"

"It's nothing. Nothing." Her heart pounded. She looked back to the waterslide.

Chloe and Christopher were still there, splashing water at each other wildly in the pool.

Oh, thank God.

"Are you sure you're all right?" Steve asked again.

Maria grabbed the drink from his hand. "I'm more than all right."

"Well, then, let's get this cruise started off right." Steve lifted his drink into the air. "Cheers to a fantastic vacation!"

Maria clinked her glass against his and took a small sip. The salt on the rim stung her tongue with an uncomfortable tang. As she swallowed, her eyes went back to the empty space on the upper deck.

"Yes. Cheers . . ."

8

The cruise ship's horn let out a long, low blast, signaling the start of its transatlantic journey. Maria unlocked a glass door, leading to her cabin's balcony, and slid it open. Hot, humid air rushed inside. Chloe and Christopher raced past her onto the balcony, taking in the glorious, summer sunshine.

The kids grabbed the rail. Stood on their tiptoes, peering out from the starboard side. Both dressed in new vacation clothes; striped T-shirts, navy shorts, brilliant white sneakers—everything but the shoes still slightly damp from their impromptu ride down the slide.

Maria loved seeing her kids like this. Fearlessly embarking on a new experience. Excitedly looking around. Glancing back to her every so often with joy in their eyes.

"Down there!" Chloe shouted. She pointed at the iconic Colgate Clock by the side of Jersey City.

"Whoa," Christopher replied. "It's huge."

"You coming out?" Steve asked from behind.

"Got a couple of things left to unpack. Gimme a sec."

"Sure thing."

Steve joined the children outside. He looked every part of his nerdy self in a T-shirt with an anchor on the front, crumpled shorts, and a pair of leather sandals. Just the way she liked him. Never out to impress. Unpretentious. Practicality and comfort always at the forefront of his mind.

The kids had grown to love him too. Maria thought the news of their engagement might distress the twins. But little did she know, Steve had already asked them for their permission before he'd even popped the question to her.

Such a gentleman.

Maria let out a satisfied sigh while watching the three of them on the balcony. She quickly grabbed everything from the suitcases that needed hanging and put them in the closet. She unloaded the wash bags and placed some of the kids' books and games on the living room table.

The two-bedroom suite had proven a wise choice.

The bathroom had enough space to dry off without banging her elbows and knees on the usual cramped surfaces. The living room had enough space to relax as a group, and they could all comfortably fit on the balcony to watch the sunset.

And the extra master bedroom meant that she and Steve could have a moment in private if the desire struck.

She placed a stack of T-shirts in a set of drawers and hung up the kids' nicer attire in the closet. Despite not having traveled in quite a while, she still moved with the efficiency of a travel pro. She zipped up the suitcases and popped them into a luggage rack by the door.

With the unpacking complete, Maria headed out onto the balcony to join her family.

She lowered her sunglasses, protecting her eyes from the intense noon glare.

The cruise ship cut through the dark blue water of the Hudson River, heading toward the Atlantic Ocean for the twelve-night cruise to England. Then they'd spend a few days in London before flying back to JFK.

"Over there!" Christopher yelled. "Is that the Statue of Liberty?"

"That's right," Steve said. "In all her copper glory."

Chloe turned. "But she's green."

"You'd be green too, if you were standing out there in the ocean for a hundred and fifty years."

Chloe slowly got the joke and let out a bellowing laugh.

Maria smiled as well. She wiped a sheen of sweat from her brow. Looked back toward the old New Jersey Railroad Terminal.

And froze.

Her smile dropped.

Her hands clamped around the balcony rail in a white-knuckled grip.

Fear shot through her body.

A lone person pushed an old-school ice cream cart along one of the five empty docks. A bit too far away to make out his face.

The ice cream cart was similar to the one Wyatt Butler allegedly used to lure in some of his young victims.

The boat had been fully boarded for hours. The docks were long since empty. No customers were around. In fact, *no one* was around at all. Not even the port security who had come to see the vessel off.

So why was this guy still pushing around an ice cream cart?

In the distance, the vendor stopped pushing the cart and looked upward at the boat as if sensing Maria's gaze.

She let out a shuddering breath and squeezed her eyes shut. Images of children's mutilated bodies flashed through her mind. Images of Wyatt Butler's face, emotionless, unfazed by the horrors.

Steve wrapped his arm around her shoulder. "Hey, love, are you sure you're okay?"

Maria opened her eyes and gazed at the dock. Like the man above the pool deck, the ice cream cart vendor had gone. She blinked hard. Scanning her eyes across the entire harbor below. But the man never reappeared.

"I . . . I'm sorry," she replied, stepping back into the room. "I saw . . . I mean I thought I saw . . . something. It's nothing."

Steve slowly shook his head. "Maria, that's twice in the past hour. I thought we stopped doing this months ago. You have to leave the case behind."

The slight twinge of disappointment in his voice hurt more than she'd expected. "I'm fine, I swear."

"Please, love, we're about to go on a really great vacation. Two weeks on the open seas—this is exactly what we need. But you have to promise me, no ghosts, okay?"

She hated admitting it, but he was right. Her sabbatical from Columbia was nearly up, and she'd be back at work again soon. But the time off had not stopped the disturbing images and thoughts. The feeling of being followed. The fear that she would be recognized and confronted, especially on a cruise ship this size, and everything would come crashing down around her once again. It took months for the constant hounding of the press to gradually fade away, and she'd spent most of the past year in self-imposed isolation. This cruise was her first real test of rejoining the world, and she already felt like she was failing.

And truthfully, she could not stop thinking about that inscription in the book . . .

You. Were. Wrong.

Steve moved closer to her as if sensing her brooding and whispered, "You're the strongest person I know. You got this."

Maria faked a smile and nuzzled her head into his shoulder.

She wanted to believe him. Desperately wanted to feel like herself again. The strength and assurance she'd once taken for granted had all but vanished. Despite everything—the press conference, the time that had passed, the sabbatical—the pain of the Butler trial still loitered in her very bones. The old Maria felt light-years away. At times, it felt like Steve was her only connection to her past self. And she hadn't even known him before the trial. She draped an arm around his chest and pulled herself in tight.

Steve returned the squeeze. But still, Maria peered through the tinted glass. Out toward the balcony.

"Now, Ms. Fontana . . . but soon to be Mrs. Brannagan . . . can I buy you another all-inclusive margarita?"

Maria kissed her fiancé on the lips and nodded.

9

Maria had told herself to get it together. Throw herself into this experience and not let anything ruin the trip. All around her, the lido deck buzzed with life. Wet footprints of scampering children had splotched across the hot wooden floor, the culprits unbothered by the lifeguard desperately yelling at them to stop running.

The area surrounding the kiddie pool was especially colorful. A group of boys wielding cheap plastic pirate swords chased a flock of screaming girls. Kids left the clown stand, clutching their new balloon animals tightly to their chests. Parents sipped at their foot-long daiquiris, willfully ignoring the chaos that surrounded them.

A bubbly announcer's voice soared out of the PA system.

"It's time for the belly-flop contest! Please come around to the booth if you'd like to participate! All ages, all bellies welcome!"

Maria managed to snag the perfect set of deck chairs close to the pool. She'd patiently waited for an elderly couple to realize that a belly-flop contest spelled the certainty of being splashed. She plopped her bag down on the rubbery chair slats and tugged at the edges of her wide-brimmed sun hat. Even out here on a crowded pool deck, being recognized by a fellow passenger's wandering eye could lead to a confrontation that Maria wanted to avoid at all costs.

I can't ruin this trip. It's gotta be perfect. For them.

With the twins splayed out in the chair next to her, Maria looked around for her safety net. He'd been following behind them just a few seconds ago.

"Where's Steve?" She nudged her daughter.

"He went that way," Chloe said, pointing to the other side of the pool deck. The kids were far more focused on the main pool where belly floppers were starting to line up.

Maria craned her neck around the deck area. No sign of Steve. She dug around in her bag, pushing aside bottle after bottle of sunscreen, and pulled out her phone. The ship had departed from port only a few hours ago. Being this close to shore, she still had a tiny bit of service. A new text from Steve appeared on her home screen.

MARGARITE FOR MY SWEET. I'LL BRB!

She typed out a message and hit Send.

YOU'RE MISSING THE BELLY FLOPS!

Maria waited for the message to go through as delivered, but the confirmation never arrived. At the top of her screen, the one bar of signal that had been clinging to life blinked out. Probably the last time she'd have service until they reached Southampton. Unless she paid an exorbitant price for cell data, which wasn't going to happen.

The announcer chimed in on the speakers.

"First up, we've got Christian Spear all the way from Pennsylvania!"

Spear walked up to the pool with a swagger and confidence he had not earned yet. The alcohol probably had a lot to do with that. He stepped out onto the diving board, shirtless, wobbly, and chugging the last of the Miller Lite in his hand. He went through a ridiculous stretching routine like he was competing in the Olympics. The audience was eating it up. Whooping and hollering cheered him on with every motion. Finally, he slapped his belly like a defiant ape and crushed the beer can against his forehead to uproarious applause.

"Ouch! That hurts!" Chloe exclaimed.

"You know it!" Maria laughed. "Just wait for this!"

The beast of a man extended his arms out to either side of him, took one deep breath, and crashed into the pool with nearly atomic force. A tsunami of water exploded out onto the deck, soaking every person, towel, and daiquiri within ten feet. Maria and her kids were drenched.

Chloe and Christopher threw their heads back and giggled with pure delight.

For the first time in a long time, Maria lay back, letting the sun dry her water-speckled skin, and smiled.

The man tightened his grip on the metal bar and pressed his body weight against the railing, trying to maintain the appearance of blending in. He was alone up here, overlooking the main deck where passengers and families had congregated for the scheduled activities of the day. He watched as a brutish, disgusting man's body slapped hard against the pool water below, sending a sting of chlorine all the way up to his elevated position.

Then he was hit by the collective laughter that followed. The sound sent a wave of revulsion through his bones that forced his muscles rigid. He breathed it in through his nostrils. Trying to savor the taste. Remember it.

A vein in his temple throbbed. He swallowed hard. Children's screams resonated through his body. Like nails down a chalkboard. Unchecked and uncontrolled by their idiot parents.

His cheeks ached from forcing fake smiles all day. He'd

nodded like an obedient dog to his fellow passengers. Had to keep up a cheery exterior, despite his revulsion at the chaos on board the ship.

He'd hated every minute since boarding in New York.

But everything had a purpose.

Michelangelo had started with a hunk of marble when creating the statue of David. Nothing started as a thing of beauty. Beauty had to be created and shaped. Natural or human forces brought about that perfection.

He lazily surveyed the deck, finally focusing upon the kiddie pool. Children screamed and played around its unhinged edges. Abandoned unicorn floaties and Nerf toys mingled on the water's surface, likely already coated in a fine layer of urine.

Disgusting.

Something by the water's edge caught his eye. A family of five had arrived late to the festivities. The two older siblings threw down their towels and dove straight into the pool to join the game of chicken that was forming.

The family's youngest son, desperate to get in on the fun, frantically jostled against his clothes. He tossed his shirt down onto the wet pool deck and kicked off his sandals in a heap. He was careless. Frantic. Only one article of his clothing made it to the deck chair.

A navy-blue New York Yankees baseball cap.

The man felt the hair on his arms bristle. The knot in his stomach loosened, and a sense of ecstasy surged through his body.

I can mold this into something perfect.

Without a second thought, he bounded down the aft stairwell and past the lido deck's bar. The late-afternoon sun was still gleaming across the Atlantic, and though he typically preferred to save this kind of activity until the cover of dusk, the events unfolding beneath him were all too good to be true.

With an opportunity like this, even he couldn't resist.

The man sidestepped around couples and retirees. He walked quickly but not too quickly, forcing a smile to please any sets of eyes that happened across him. The kiddie pool was now only a few steps to his left.

He stepped over a wet towel and swiped the Yankees hat in one swift motion, imperceptibly shoving it into his pocket among the hundreds of parents and children that swarmed around him. Next, he ducked back into the aft hallway, past the bar, and into the men's bathroom.

No one at the urinals.

Crouching down low, he swept his head across each stall, searching for feet.

Empty.

He squeezed himself into one of the narrow stalls and slammed the door shut with a clang. Pulled the hat from his pocket and gently ran his thumb across the embroidered logo. Each white thread prickled the sensors in his skin. He flipped the cap over, examining every inch of the inside, still warm from the heat of the child's head.

He ran his pinkie along the brim, then rubbed that same finger along the outside of his lips. The bathroom door rattled, breaking up his thoughts. Someone else had entered. The man stuffed the cap back into his pocket and grabbed at the toilet paper dispenser. He curled a wad of tissue around his hand and gingerly depressed the toilet handle, allowing the sound of the flush to engulf the room.

Moments later, he faked a cough, then stepped out of the stall.

And came face-to-face with the passenger who'd just entered.

This man stood a few inches shorter than he. Young. Perhaps even a teenager. His mouth hung open in a sluggish gape. The acne along his chin blistering red. Made worse by the new sunburn sinking into his skin. He stumbled toward the automatic sink and stuck his head under the water.

Drunk.

The short man vomited whatever bright red frozen cocktail he'd been drinking and slumped over on the counter.

Idiot.

Feeling that the hat was still safely stowed in his pocket,

the man shook his head in revulsion. Stepped out of the bathroom—disappearing back into the crowded mass of passengers.

Attempting to blend in, while holding his new prize close to his body . . .

10

The sun had set over the Atlantic, and stars filled the clear night sky. A visibly annoyed Pam Mayer sat perched on the end of her cabin's bed, glaring over the vast, inky black ocean. It had been two hours since she'd last phoned reception and complained about the terrible stench. Yet nobody had come up, and it was getting worse, day after day.

So bad that her eyes watered.

She punched the comforter in frustration.

A thousand bucks a night, my ass.

This was only day number five of the cruise. Barely halfway across the Atlantic Ocean. There was no way in hell Pam was going to tolerate this smell for another seven days. If she'd wanted that, she could have stayed in Jersey and saved the cash.

In the corridor, an electronic pad beeped.

The cabin entrance swung open, and her husband, Larry, entered, holding a key card in one hand and a plate of cheese fries in the other, seemingly oblivious to the odor.

"Well?" Pam snapped.

"Well, what?"

"What did they say? I take it you went to reception again like I asked?"

Larry avoided eye contact. He sat with his back to her, licking the cheese off his fingers.

Pam shuffled closer to him. "You didn't go, did you?"

"I didn't forget. I just . . . thought you'd want the fries while they're hot. I'll go right after this."

"Goddamn it, Larry." Pam grabbed the plate from his lap and poured the fries into the small garbage bin by the bed. "You bring a tray of cheese fries into our room that already stinks to high heavens?"

"Hey," Larry protested. "What the hell, Pam?"

"I'm not spending another minute in here. I'm not having our entire vacation ruined because all you can think about are french fries. I'll be right back."

Pam grabbed a chiffon cover-up from the closet and wrapped it around her bathing suit. She slipped her feet into a pair of flip-flops, swept the key card off the dresser, and headed out of the cabin.

She strode along the corridor. The smiles on the faces of other passengers she passed only enraged her further.

Yeah. That's right. I bet you're all having a great *time.*

Of course we get the goddamned smelly cabin.

She descended in the elevator, eyes thinned, focused on her mission. The question was—how curt should she be? It depended on how she was treated. On how seriously the cruise ship took their customer service. She wasn't going to settle for anything less than a profuse apology and potentially even a partial refund. A full refund if they couldn't fix the smell or find them a new cabin.

The car bumped to a stop and let out a polite chime. She burst out as soon as the doors parted and headed directly toward the crewmember behind the reception desk.

He met her with a smile that she didn't return.

"Hi there. Can I help you, ma'am?"

"I wanted you to help me two hours ago. Pam Mayer, room 819."

The receptionist tapped something on his keyboard. Pursed his lips. "Ah yes. Mrs. Mayer. Someone from maintenance will be up to your room shortly to check on your leak."

"It's not a leak, *Drew,*" she shot back, reading his name tag. "It's a God-awful smell. And I've been waiting for two hours."

"I understand, and I'm so sorry for the wait. You have my word, we'll have your cabin checked within the hour."

Pam shook her head. Any more of this condescending treatment would make her head explode. She took four soothing breaths. But even the twenty yoga classes she'd taken last year couldn't help her now. "I've already told you, the problem is not coming from my cabin. It's coming from next door. Room 817."

He tapped on his keyboard a few more times. "Are you sure?" His eyes scanned down the hundreds of rows' worth of cabin data. "Room 817 is unoccupied, so it's highly unlikely that—"

"It's 817," Pam replied abruptly. "We've been through this already. I've talked to three different versions of you, Drew. There's an adjoining door to our cabin. The terrible smell is coming from there."

"You're sure?"

"Positive. Now will you please pick up the phone and light a fire under someone's ass?"

The receptionist smirked and raised the phone to his ear and hit a few buttons to dial. He spoke in hushed tones for a minute, then gave her that same canned smile again. "Mrs. Mayer, we'll have someone from maintenance up to your room immediately. Please return to meet her there."

"Thank you."

Pam spun away and headed out of the reception area. A few people in proximity gave her an odd look. The angry scowl on her face stuck out like a sore thumb among the dozens of carefree passengers passing by the reception desk.

Whatever. If they had the same problem in their cabins, they'd be pissed too.

In this world, there were people that got pushed around, and then there were those that did the pushing. She smiled to herself and headed back to the cabin.

Back on the eighth floor, she entered the room.

Larry had grabbed a can of Bud from the minibar. He lowered it from his lips when she entered, looking guilty of something. "How'd it go?"

"They'll be here in a minute."

"Great," he replied, pulling Pam close. "Hey, I'm sorry I didn't take care of it like you asked. I promise that I'll make it up to you after dinner." He winked not very subtly.

"Oh, you're gonna put in the work, all right," she replied, winking back.

The moment would've been sweet had it not been for the noxious smell of the room that'd once again commandeered Pam's nostrils.

A moment later, someone knocked on the cabin door.

"Finally!" Pam said. She raced over and flung it open.

A woman stood waiting, dressed in a cream coverall with a tool belt. "Hi, I hear you've got a problem in the room?"

"It's a smell coming from next door."

"Do you mind if I come in and check things out?"

Pam extended her palm toward the living area. "Please! Save our vacation."

The woman moved around the area. First, she checked inside the cramped bathroom. Then the minibar. Then around the bed. Something beneath the bedside table caught her eye.

"Well, you've got a pile of cheese fries here in your trash."

"No, no." Pam waved her off. "I just put those in there. And you think *that* smell is cheese fries? Have you ever smelled cheese fries before? It's coming from next door."

"I see."

Pam stood waiting by the locked internal door that led to the next cabin, tapping her foot impatiently.

Eventually, after a few more moments of searching the Mayers' room, the maintenance woman joined her.

"Believe me now?" Pam asked.

"Yep, you're right. Your cabin is a-okay. It's coming from this door connecting you to the next room."

"No shit."

The woman fished a bunch of keys from her belt, sorted through them until she found the right one. She poked it into the cabin's connector door lock and twisted. Pam stood by her shoulder, waiting for her to open it. Wanted to see whatever had created the stench.

Oh, we're definitely getting this leg of the trip for free. At least a discount, especially if I post it on Yelp.

"Mind moving back so I can open the door?" the woman asked.

Pam took two steps back.

The woman opened the door, revealing the empty, pitch-black adjoining cabin.

A far stronger smell blasted out of the dark space, immediately overwhelming and shocking Pam's senses.

It was putrid. Something rotten.

Like a decomposing animal.

The maintenance woman was also taken aback by the smell. She reached her hand inside, felt along the wall, and hit a light switch. Then she let out a piercing, bloodcurdling scream.

Pam peered over the woman's shoulder at the sight and nearly fainted. But she remained on her feet, and her scream rang out just as loudly as she emptied her lungs.

"My . . . God," Larry murmured.

The three of them stood there, staring at the bed in the adjoining room. Frozen. In a state of complete, unadulterated shock.

Staring at the most horrific thing Pam had ever seen in her entire life.

11

The phone rang on the wall of the operations room on the tenth deck. Jake Reese, the ship's head of security, spun his chair away from the array of monitoring screens and rolled across the room to grab the receiver. Before he could say hello, the pager on his belt beeped, demanding his attention as well.

Something was going down.

Reese planted the phone to his ear. "Security," he answered. "Jake Reese speaking."

"It's Drew from reception," a frantic voice replied. "You need to get to room 817. I repeat, 817. Please. Right now."

"Calm down, Drew. What's happened?"

"Maintenance has discovered a . . . a body," the receptionist stammered.

He straightened in his chair. "Got it. Now, follow your training, Drew, and stay calm. Have medical meet me there. We're on our way."

"No, you don't understand—" Drew said as Reese hung the phone up, cutting him off.

Reese shook his head at his second-in-command, Tracy Hendricks. He let out a long sigh. *Just my luck. Right when I thought we might be in the clear.*

"What's happening?" Hendricks asked.

"Dead passenger in one of the rooms."

"Oh, jeez." Hendricks bowed her head and let out a sigh of her own. "Probably some underlying medical condition, like usual."

"No doubt about that," he agreed. "The way the guy at reception sounded on the phone, you'd think no one ever died on a cruise ship before."

These types of incidents were not rare on a ship this size. In his entire cruise career, Reese had probably seen a hundred dead bodies, and almost all were from natural causes. Not to mention the passengers that fell overboard, which happened far more frequently than the public knew. Almost always a result of intoxication.

Reese pulled two Glocks from the safe, more from habit than necessity. He handed one to Hendricks, which she immediately holstered. Realistically, this was going to be the medical team's show, but Reese went through the motions nonetheless.

"All right, let's check it out."

Reese had twelve years' worth of experience as a cop in the Miami Police Department. Over a decade on cruise ships too. Hendricks was his number two for only a few years, but she was his best asset. Her heart was in the job, he could feel it. They both liked what they did. And more importantly, he trusted her. Which was more than he could say about a lot of the cops he'd worked with back on the force.

They headed out into one of the concealed walkways that ran between every floor. Hustled along the plain, light blue corridor. He called two of his team on his walkie-talkie, asking them to meet him at the cabin. Hendricks and Reese clambered down two flights of stairs to the eighth level, and he pushed his way through one of the emergency exit doors.

A couple stood only a few feet away. A woman in a bathing suit and chiffon, and her husband in a Hawaiian shirt and bright shorts. She had tears in her eyes. He had a comforting arm around her, and they headed away from room 817.

"Are you guys okay?" Hendricks asked.

"What do you think?" the woman said, her voice cracking. "We were next door."

Hendricks directed the couple toward the end of the corridor where a few of the staff had arrived. Whatever they'd seen, the crewmembers from the customer service team were more than equipped to handle it. The cruise line had made sure of that. Especially in recent years. An army of corporate lawyers, layered protocols, and mountains of NDA paperwork would ensure that nothing they'd seen would ever reach the prying eyes of the press.

Reese advanced toward the room. The familiar scent he'd encountered hundreds of times drifted by through the air all around him from farther down the hall. Unmistakable.

A maintenance woman stood outside the now open door of room 817, clutching her nose in a tight-pinched grip. "It's in here," she said.

He nodded an acknowledgment. As he crossed through the doorway, the distinct odor of human decomposition invaded his nostrils. Reese glanced over his shoulder at Hendricks. She returned his grim look.

From the smell alone, Reese could tell that the death was not a recent one. His experience told him that the passenger had been dead for some time.

Reese stepped into the bedroom and froze.

"Jesus Christ," he muttered.

Hendricks abruptly stopped by his side. "What the hell . . . ," she said, covering her mouth, trying desperately not to gag.

A severed human head had been meticulously placed in the center of the bed. Male. Wearing a pair of circular glasses; the left lens shattered. Lips slightly parted. No visible blood in the room at all.

And no body.

No way this was natural causes.

This was . . .

Reese took a moment to compose himself, remembering that he'd just stepped foot onto the crime scene. No need to jump to any conclusions just yet.

A few other items had been placed on the bedsheet, but they could wait for the moment. First, Reese needed to take immediate action. He briskly headed back into the hallway.

Two of his team had arrived outside. Two young men, hired by Hendricks. Men she trusted. Reese knew they had no experience in this type of situation, but they just might be good enough to keep everyone at bay while he carried out his initial investigation.

"Clear all the cabins on this corridor *now,*" Reese ordered. "Let's relocate these passengers elsewhere on the ship. Tell them they got upgraded or some shit. Then, seal off this level, and don't allow anyone inside this room without my permission."

"Everyone?" one of them asked.

"Everyone. Including staff. Until further notice. And not a word of this spreads, not from us and not from the passengers who saw this, understood? We don't need panic, and even more importantly, we don't need rumors."

Reese returned back inside. Realistically, his team had no forensic capabilities beyond the naked eye and photographic evidence. All they could do was capture and preserve the scene and hopefully ascertain who the victim was. As for apprehending the perpetrator of this crime, well . . . this wasn't the Miami Police Department, and he knew it. Running any kind of fingerprint or blood analysis on this ship was out of the question.

The captain would demand answers, and Reese had better have some quickly.

Back in the room, Hendricks had already slapped on latex gloves and was accessing the ship's maintenance and passenger logs on her tablet.

Reese zipped open his daypack. He slid his hands into his own pair of gloves and pulled out the still camera. He moved closer to the bed and began to slowly snap photos of the gruesome scene.

He pressed his handkerchief to his face and breathed through his mouth to avoid taking in the sickly stench.

The severed head had signs of decomposition with considerable marbling of the skin and grossly swollen features. If Reese had to guess, he'd say maybe a week old. That meant it could have been placed here just before they set sail.

"Who is the occupant of this room?" Reese asked.

"Manifest says the room is empty," Hendricks replied, looking through the database. "And the room was last serviced before passengers boarded six days ago, nothing unusual in the report."

"I want to speak to whomever serviced the room last, and the floor supervisor. And I want a report of any master key cards that have gone missing. *Someone* got into this room and staged this here, and I want to find out who."

"Understood," Hendricks replied.

"Let's pull security footage too. As far back as we can go. I want to see everyone who's been in and out of this room from the last ten days. Even if it's footage from the ship's previous voyage."

She nodded and put out the call on her walkie to the team who'd covered for them in the operations room.

Reese crouched by the side of the bed. Slowly edged closer to the head.

Several tendons at the bottom of the neck had been tied in a neat bow, as if at the bottom of a laced shoe, and had left no signs of errant viscera. Whoever did this macabre act had done so after death, and possibly after exsanguinating the body.

Reese shuddered.

He'd only ever seen pictures of this. Heard stories from the old-school guys in Miami from serial killer murder scenes. Somebody had gone to a lot of effort to create this tableau.

A child's Yankees baseball cap sat squarely next to the right ear.

The head was clearly an adult male. The goatee, wrinkles, and sprinkling of gray hairs made it obvious. So why the child's cap?

On the other side of the bed was an old-school typewriter. An Olympia with an army-green coat of paint and pristine keys. For Reese, a bizarre item he'd never seen on a cruise ship before. Even the mere existence of the object seemed strange to him.

Obsolete.

Reese leaned over and snapped another photo. "There's something written on the page."

He peered down at the single piece of paper, protruding from the machine.

If the judicial system can't stop him, who will?

The message was typed out in intentional clacking keystrokes. Each letter was perfect. No hint of Wite-Out in sight.

"What the hell does that mean?" Hendricks asked, peering over his shoulder.

"We are being toyed with. Let's do a ship-wide roll call, both crew and passengers. Find out who's missing, and we'll know who this guy is. And then hopefully, who put him here."

12

A neutral voice repeatedly boomed over the public address system. Maria grabbed Chloe and Christopher by the hand, and they paused outside the movie theater entrance. Other passengers had also stopped, appearing as equally as confused by the ship's abrupt announcement.

"Attention, all passengers. Please proceed to your assigned emergency station for a mandatory roll call. Crewmembers will be opening all quarters to help assist everyone to their designated stations. Thank you for your prompt assistance."

A woman, who was with a young boy, glanced across to Maria. "Why do they need a roll call?"

She shrugged. "Beats me."

"You think someone's missing?"

"I guess we'll find out when we get there." She peered down at the children with a sympathetic smile. "This won't take long, guys. We just need to let the crew know we're safe and well."

"But we'll miss the movie," Christopher complained.

"They'll wait for us. Or we'll catch it tomorrow."

"What about Steve?" Chloe asked.

"I'm sure he'll meet us there, honey. Now let's get moving."

Steve had stayed in the cabin to take a nap. He was a light sleeper, so she had no worries.

She gripped the kids' hands tighter as they headed along the walkway toward the stairs. The number of people around them quickly swelled. Passengers had left the theater, their cabins, the pool, the buffet. Everything emptied out quickly.

The crowd streamed down the staircase toward the vast ballroom, which was one of the designated meeting stations. More joined from every level, mirroring the drill they'd carried out when first boarding the ship. The overriding sense around her was one of irritation. Complaints about the timing. Unfounded rumors that a kid probably lost his or her parents, which Maria had to imagine was fairly common.

Maria and the kids headed for their muster point at the back left of the ballroom. The crewmember representative, wearing a luminous orange vest, stood waiting with a clipboard.

Maria breathed a sigh of relief when her eyes met Steve's. He'd already arrived and was leaning against one of the fake Roman columns.

"Hey, Steve," Christopher said.

"Hey, little buddy."

Steve bumped his fists with the kids'. His idea of acting cool.

Maria headed over to the rep. "Cabin 925. The Fontana family. All four of us are here."

The rep scanned down the clipboard with his pen, locating their cabin number on his document. He eyed Steve for a moment, then scored out their names on the paper. "Okay, thanks very much, folks. You're good to go."

"That's it?"

"Yep, thanks for coming so fast."

"Can I ask why you're doing this?"

"Oh, I assure you, there's nothing to worry about. It's a pretty standard roll call."

"But six days into the cruise?" Maria asked. "Is that standard? Is someone missing?"

He shook his head. "No, no, nothing like that. Now please, Ms. Fontana, go back to enjoying the cruise."

Maria studied his face for a second until he turned away. The crewmember appeared genuine in his response. Everything seemed casual enough, though it still didn't explain the strangeness of a mid-cruise roll call. She weaved through the crowd back toward Steve.

And froze when something caught her ear. Nearby, a group of five women, looking in their late twenties and very clearly intoxicated, excitedly shared what they'd heard around the ship. Maria strained to eavesdrop on their conversation.

"—found a decapitated head, positioned on the bed, but no body," one woman whispered. "And not only that. There was no blood."

"How's that possible?" another woman asked.

"Beats the hell outta me. The woman in the cabin next door found it in an empty room. Someone heard her talking to security."

"Do they think it was an accident? Or murder?"

"Are you kidding? Who accidentally decapitates themselves on a cruise ship? In their own cabin?"

Throughout this fevered speculation, Maria's heart rate had spiked. She drew in a sharp breath. From the little details she could hear—which she assumed were almost entirely hearsay—the apparent discovery sounded horrifically familiar.

Just like what Wyatt Butler was accused of doing to so many of those innocent children.

Stop, Maria.

You're being paranoid again.

She headed back over to Steve and the kids, debating whether to report back to him privately what she had overheard.

"Maria, is everything okay?" he asked. "You look like you've seen a ghost."

"I'm fine. Just drunken rumors. Not worth repeating."

He rested a hand on her shoulder. "Why don't we head back to the cabin, wait for everything to calm down a little bit. We can plan out tonight. Sound good?"

Maria smiled. "That's good with me."

Anything to keep from being alone with her thoughts right now . . .

Jake Reese circled the queen-size bed again, staring at the decapitated head, the Yankees baseball cap, and the typewriter. His team had found no other visual evidence—no forced entry, not a single thing out of place in the room, nothing else disturbed in the slightest. In all his years of experience on land and at sea, he'd never come across such a macabre and strange scene. This rivaled the most brutal drug-related revenge killings he'd seen during his time on the force in Miami. Since they were nearly at the halfway point in their journey, Reese assumed the captain would continue going forward to Southampton and let the authorities investigate the crime when they arrived. Until then, his job was to preserve the evidence and make sure no one else on board the ship was in danger. And the first step was finding out who this person was.

Hendricks walked back into the cabin. "Jake, the ship-wide roll call is complete."

"And?" Reese asked.

"And you're never gonna believe this."

"Try me."

"All passengers on board are accounted for. All crewmembers are accounted for. No one is missing, not a single person." Hendricks shrugged. "So it seems we have a stowaway."

"Someone who snuck on board the ship? Got past security and immigration? I suppose that's possible."

Reese scratched his head, pondering the circumstances.

"Either that, or someone brought this on board for us to find," he added. "A souvenir, if you will."

"This case is getting more bizarre by the minute."

"Tell me about it," Reese replied. "Let me ask you a question. If no one is missing on board this ship, then how the hell do we find out who this guy is?"

13

The sun dipped behind a puffy white cloud. Maria rolled to the side on her lounger and checked her watch. It was close to mid-day. An hour before the kids' magic show in the forward bar. Steve lay on a lounger by her side, reading a creature-feature horror novel. Several feet to their front, Chloe and Christopher had made friends and played by the edge of the pool.

On the surface, everything was bliss.

"How's the book?" she asked Steve.

"Pretty good. It's about a prehistoric arachnid hunting campers. Right up your alley." He rolled toward Maria. "It feels a bit weird down here today, don't you think?"

"How do you mean?"

"Subdued. Like . . . I don't know. Quieter than yesterday."

Maria scanned the pool area, trying to take in the atmosphere on the boat. Sure, it wasn't as busy as yesterday. Maybe the cooler temperature in the mid-Atlantic. Whatever the reason, she noticed the muted atmosphere as well. She had tried to ignore it in case it triggered her paranoia.

"Yeah, you're right," she said.

"With all the rumors going around the ship since that drill last night, maybe people are spooked. I dunno."

"Jeez, Steve. You sound worse than I do."

"I'm just saying. You know what I mean?"

"Can't believe I'm the one saying this, but let's not get paranoid."

He let out a belly laugh and gave Maria a kiss on the lips. "You're right, Ms. Fontana. You're almost always right."

"Almost?" she coyly shot back. "Wanna drink?"

"Sure. Is it too early for a vodka and Sprite?"

She smiled at his mock-concerned face. "What was it you said last week? London time, baby!"

Maria sprang from the lounger, wrestled on her T-shirt, and headed inside to the bar. Even though she hid it well, she could not stop thinking about what Steve had said and those horrible rumors that had been spreading like wildfire. Those chilling claims she had overheard last night. A passenger decapitated. No body. No blood.

The terrifying rumor was so oddly . . . specific.

Maria let out a deep sigh as she entered the bar. There were only a few people waiting for service.

She spied the area, secretly checking out her fellow passengers from behind the safety of her sunglasses. Analyzing each one, studying their features, looking for anything unusual or out of place. Then she remembered one of the curious details from the trial. A detail that cast doubt on the prosecution's entire case against Wyatt Butler.

Every eyewitness police sketch of the serial killer looked completely different. Different hair, different eyes, height, weight, age. Multiple children were murdered in the exact same way, but the various police sketches of the suspected killer looked nothing alike. Maria could be standing next to the real killer on board this ship, and she wouldn't even know.

The prosecution had no good explanation for this glaring discrepancy.

A member of the security team crossed the bar area. A woman who looked like a stern version of Kelly Clarkson, dressed in a dark blue polo and matching shorts. She moved with purpose, heading toward the staircase.

Maria stepped away from the bar and met her halfway across the room. She needed to know more about last night's events.

The woman locked eyes with her as Maria stepped across her path. "Can I help you, ma'am?"

"Uh, yes. My name is Maria, and I was wondering if I could ask you a couple of questions."

"Sure. How can I help?"

Maria glanced down at the woman's name badge. "Ms. Hendricks, I was wondering if you could tell me why we had the roll call last night."

"It's nothing for you to worry about."

"That's not what I'm asking."

"Ma'am—"

"Please, call me Maria."

Hendricks gave a resigned nod. "Hello, Maria. There's nothing to worry about. Everyone on the ship is accounted for."

Maria edged closer. Glanced around to check if everyone else in the bar was out of earshot. "And how about the man who was decapitated? Is he accounted for as well?"

Hendricks's false smile vanished quickly. "If I were you, I'd ignore speculation and keep those kind of stories to yourself. Keep in mind that the only things on board that move faster than the cruise ship are rumors."

"Please, I'm a psychologist. The reason I approached is to offer my services. If anyone on board needs help or is going through trauma of some kind—"

"We'll be sure to know where to find you."

With her interruption complete, Hendricks circled Maria and continued on her way, dismissing the entire encounter.

The abrupt ending of the meeting hardly eased Maria's

concerns. If anything, Hendricks's evasiveness had only heightened her suspicions that something bad had happened last night.

A middle-aged man with bloodshot eyes directly approached from the bar. His long, scraggly beard covered a ketchup-stained Iron Man T-shirt. He pointed his shot glass in the direction of Hendricks. "Did she tell you anything?"

"No."

"Yeah, me neither. Spoke to her an hour ago. Pretty useless."

Maria nodded, while slowly backing away from the stench of stale booze. "Anyway, it was nice meeting you."

She spun to walk away. Steve's drinks could wait. She wanted to know more, but not from the ship's drunk.

"Did you hear about his neck?" the man called after her, slurring his words.

Maria turned around, caught off guard by the question.

The man slurred, "I heard from one of the people on the same floor. Whoever decapitated the guy tied everything together into a neat little bow. All the tendons. What sick fuck would do that?"

Maria's limbs froze in shock at what she had just heard. The answer was obvious.

Finally, she spun away and rapidly made her way back to her lounge chair, fighting off a full panic attack.

"No drink?" Steve asked as she sat down.

Maria ignored the question and let the drunk passenger's words sink in.

Tied into a little bow . . .

All the tendons . . .

All the images came rushing back to her. And in her mind's eye, she was back inside the courtroom.

"Your Honor, we'd like to move on to the presentation of evidence."

For the trial of Wyatt Butler, the State of New York had pulled out all the stops. The prosecuting lawyer in this case was Edward "the Killer" Kohl, a man who would've been attorney general if it weren't for some high-class nepotism happening in Albany. Ironic that the self-proclaimed Killer would now be the one to prosecute possibly the country's worst serial offender, a detail the national tabloid headline writers delighted in.

"Ladies and gentlemen of the jury, please direct your attention to the screen here," Mr. Kohl requested. "And bear in mind these are sensitive materials that some may find disturbing—an unfortunate disclaimer that speaks directly to the heinous and downright evil acts Mr. Butler has committed."

The screen flickered to life with the nightmarish image that was Exhibit A.

Sharp gasps punctured the courtroom's silence. Though the judge hadn't allowed any news reporters or journalists into the trial, the civilians who had gotten seats were apt to vocalize. After the first few days of the trial, it became clear to Maria which victims' families were in attendance. Her heart broke hearing their gasps.

"Order!" the judge commanded, banging her gavel.

"Thank you, Your Honor. As shown here, Exhibit A depicts what remained of Mr. Butler's third alleged victim, Kaitlyn Broderick. Six years old at the time of her disappearance and subsequent murder. She was last seen leaving school on the night of . . ."

His voice drowned away in Maria's ears. The image that still blazed across the screen was boring a hole through her pupils, a hole not even her eyelids dared to block out. She couldn't move. She felt paralyzed—experiencing just a tiny fraction of the death this little girl had viciously suffered through alone.

In the gruesome crime scene photo, the little girl was forced to kneel on the floor in an abandoned log cabin. Six-inch nails had been hammered through her feet and knees to keep her legs in place. A steel rod kept her back straight and her body unnaturally upright like a mannequin. The killer had dressed her in a boy's denim overalls, two sizes too big for her. Her arms had been removed and placed in front of her. And her eyelids propped open, as if the child were looking down upon her own death.

Whatever monster had done this to her left no part undisturbed. Even her hair. Her brown braids had been chopped off at the scalp and purposefully woven into braids left neatly on the floor, in perfectly arranged circles.

But most sickening and disturbing of all was the little girl's neck and head, which had been separated from her body and hung down from a rope attached to the ceiling. Gently swaying above the tableau.

One would expect blood. And lots of it. But there was none at the scene. Instead, her carotid artery and jugular veins had been fastened together into a bow—pink and orderly. As if she were finally wearing an accessory she'd wanted for Christmas.

Maria held back the urge to vomit. Others in the courtroom were not so lucky . . .

Maria's mind snapped back to the present.

The sun still shone down from the clear blue sky, and her kids yelped with excitement as they played by the pool. But Maria remained consumed in her own thoughts. Frozen.

All these similarities to the case . . .

This can't be happening.

Can it?

14

Ten-year-old Owen Daley fought off sleep as best he could. His parents had already gone to bed in their cabin. Once he made sure they were asleep, his plan was to swipe the key card out of his mom's lanyard and head straight for the basketball court. A quiet area near the back of the ship, and he was betting the court would be empty.

He stared at the digital clock. Nearly eleven at night and the rest of the passengers would be in the ballroom singing karaoke or drinking. The sound from the party reverberated across the open-air decks of the ship, getting louder each time someone walked through the automatic sliding-glass doors to head back to their rooms.

Owen stifled a yawn. Some good had to come out of this

day. After losing a game of chicken in the pool to a girl earlier in the afternoon, he was determined to make a few baskets before going to sleep.

Now was the time to make a break for it.

Owen swept the comforter to one side.

Crept to the door. Slowly opened it. Winced as it creaked. Stepped into the dim corridor and closed the cabin.

He waited for a moment, listening intently for any signs of his parents scrambling out of bed. Nothing. Then he moved off at a fast walk. Rushed up the staircase to the right deck and headed toward the door.

An old couple headed toward him.

Owen looked down, avoiding eye contact as he made it outside.

The wind had picked up. It blew hard across the ship, through his thin green T-shirt, and sent a shiver up his spine. He jogged along the deserted walkway toward the back of the ship. Farther away from the sounds of the partying. Closer to his own quiet space to have some fun.

Owen found the court empty.

A smile stretched across his face as he headed inside.

The basketballs had been stowed away by the maintenance staff for the night, but Owen spotted a forgotten one tucked under a bench. The ball was slightly deflated from the wear and tear of the day. He didn't mind. The little bit of extra give meant he could get a better grip with his small hands.

He tossed the ball toward the hoop. It clattered off the rim and shot back toward him.

A voice cut through the echoing bounces of the ball. "Tough shot, but you're pretty good."

Owen spun around, startled at the sounds of a spectator.

A man stood with his hands clutching the chain-link fence that surrounded the court.

"Mind if I come watch?" the man asked.

Owen turned back toward the hoop, too tired and too uninterested to respond. He'd had his cheeks pinched too many times today by his parents' dumb friends to let this adult bother him now.

The man squeezed himself between the opening of the fence and walked over to where Owen dribbled. "I gotta tell ya. I love sports too. What's your favorite?"

The boy weighed his options. "Baseball," he finally replied.

The man laughed. "Baseball, huh? Me too! Let me guess . . . Do you like the Yankees?"

"Yeah! I love the Yankees!" Owen grinned, showing off the gap where his front tooth was still missing. "I lost my favorite Yankees hat today, though. My mom got so mad."

"Aw, that's a shame. I'm sure it'll turn up somewhere. What's your name?"

"Owen."

"No way! Are you serious? *My* name's Owen too!" the man said with a warm grin.

The boy looked up at him with one eyebrow raised. "Really?"

"Yep. Been my name my whole life."

Owen smiled at the man's joke.

"How old are you?"

Owen took another shot at the basketball hoop. It awkwardly hit the backboard and bounced back toward the middle of the court, sending him sprinting after it.

The man positioned himself beneath the basket. "I bet you're at least twelve, right?"

"Ten!"

"Ten! Wow, you look older," the man replied. "Ten, now that's a good number. Like Phil Rizzuto."

Owen smiled at the mention of the legendary Yankees ballplayer. He dribbled the ball by his side, lined up another shot, and chucked it toward the hoop.

The ball soared through the air just short of the rim.

The man caught it just before it hit the ground. He dribbled the ball back toward Owen and said, "I bet you'll be tall when you grow up. Probably tall enough to be a great pitcher."

"My brother makes fun of me for being short. He's taller than me, but that's because he's older. But our sister is even taller than him! She's the oldest."

"Well, I bet she can't dunk a basketball. But I bet you can."

"What? No way! I can't do that!" Owen laughed. "My dad

says maybe when I'm older. He thinks I'll be at least six foot when I'm fifteen."

"Well, who's got time to wait until you're fifteen? Here, come over here. I'll pick you up, and you can dunk it through the hoop. It'll be awesome."

"Uh." Owen looked down at the laces on his tennis shoes. This man seemed nice, but . . . "It's okay. I'll just shoot some hoops."

"C'mon, how cool would it be if you dunk one shot? Ten bucks says you can do it."

He looked at the man, who smiled back at him with open arms, and then up at the hoop.

Owen really wanted to make a basket.

"Just one?" the man pressed.

"Uh, okay," Owen replied.

He headed over to the nice man. Someone whom he had lots in common with.

With one quick scoop, the man lifted Owen beneath the armpits and propped him up by the hoop. Even with the boost, Owen's arms were still a bit too short. He struggled to push the ball above the rim. Grunted with effort. But it was no use.

Then the man took a step back, away from the hoop.

The basketball tumbled out of Owen's hand and hit the court with a smack.

"Hey! I didn't do it yet!" Owen cried out. "Let me try again!"

The man ignored him. He walked backward toward the court exit, carrying the boy firmly in his arms.

Owen laughed at first, reminded of the many times his own father had picked him up like this and spun him around. But this wasn't the same.

The man stepped through the fence and carried him onto the open-air deck.

Sensing the danger, Owen began to struggle. "Hey! Put me down!" He kicked his legs against the man's chest. "Put me *down*!"

The man tightened his grip on the boy and peered out across the rough water. No stars shone that night. Only the light of the half-moon twinkled on the tips of the water.

With one final heave, the man lifted the boy above his head and tossed him over the guard railing.

Owen screamed all the way down until his body smashed against the freezing surface of the pitch-black Atlantic Ocean.

15

A fist banged on the operations room door.

Reese had just come off a long security briefing with his team and an even longer call with the cruise line's crisis management office. He'd put the word out to his staff that he was not to be disturbed.

Pain throbbed in his head. A growing migraine for sure. He stared at his reflection in the monitor's dark face. A vein bulged along the center of his forehead.

The knock came again.

"Come in!" Reese finally said, annoyed.

Two figures entered the room. One was Leah, the head of guest services. She'd organized the roll call and had been quick on her feet when Reese needed her most.

"I'm sorry, Mr. Reese, but we have a guest here. This is Mrs. Rebecca Daley. She wants to speak with you. Her son's gone missing."

Reese stood from his desk and motioned for Mrs. Daley to take a seat.

The woman had a red face and puffy eyes from crying. She wore a set of silk pajamas. Reese glanced at the clock on the wall.

2:16 in the morning.

He reached into his filing drawer and pulled out the missing minor form. "Hi, Rebecca, please call me Jake," Reese said softly. "Can you tell me what happened?"

"We can't find my son. My husband and I. Please, if there's anything you can do to help."

"I promise we will. What's your son's name?"

"Owen."

Reese went through the rest of the form, getting the boy's age, height, weight, description, and information pertinent to his last known whereabouts. Children went "missing" on cruise ships all the time. In fact, Reese couldn't recall the last time he'd gone an entire voyage without at least one scare. Most of the time, the kids had wandered off to the bathroom alone or found a good spot for a game of hide-and-seek. At more than a thousand feet long and three hundred feet high, there were a lot of places for kids to get lost on the *Atlantia*.

"Have you looked in the arcade? Lots of kids like to sneak away there. It's open all night."

"Yes, we've looked everywhere. Please, my husband's out there running around like a madman looking for him. We woke up two hours ago, and he wasn't in bed—"

Reese carefully weighed his options. To put out a missing child announcement ship-wide across the PA system, at this hour of the morning, would wake up and possibly upset a fair amount of passengers. With all the rumors circulating about the earlier incident, he had to stay extra levelheaded. Then again, given the day's gruesome discovery on board, it couldn't hurt to be extra careful.

"How about this, Mrs. Daley—I'll put in a call to my team to conduct a ship-wide search. While they're doing that, I'll review the security camera footage, and let's see if we can track down where Owen went. Honestly, he likely just snuck out to meet some other kids or is probably eating ice cream at the buffet as we speak. Rest assured, we'll find him for you."

She sniffled into her tissue and nodded.

Reese unclipped his walkie-talkie from his belt and brought it up to his mouth. "Hendricks, come in, Hendricks."

Tracy's voice crackled in a few seconds later. "Go for Hendricks."

"We have a missing child from room 536. Name is Owen Daley. Caucasian, age ten, four feet, nine inches. Last seen on the fifth floor at 10:00 p.m. wearing a green T-shirt and shorts."

"Copy that. We're already on it. Found an article of children's clothing by the basketball court. Bringing it to your office now."

"Ten-four. See you soon."

Mrs. Daley looked up at Reese with a glimmer of hope in her eyes. "Clothing? Did they find his shirt? Is that good news?" She spoke quickly.

Could be. Could be nothing.

"We'll let you identify it and go from there, Rebecca," Reese replied reassuringly. "But I think we found our culprit—the old late-night basketball game when no parents are around. Happens all the time." Reese smiled at the concerned mother.

Indeed, it was fairly common. No matter how much the ship tried, kids always found a way to sneak onto the courts in the middle of the night. He supposed late-night hoops was a better alternative than other troubles kids could be getting into.

Reese rolled back in his chair over to the security computer and pulled up the grid of camera feeds. He reversed the playback time to 10:00 p.m. and began scrolling through each system floor by floor.

Nothing.

He zeroed in on the fifth-floor cameras and pinpointed the view of cabin 536.

There.

The grainy video showed Owen Daley leaving the stateroom at 10:51 p.m., completely alone. Reese clicked on the camera feeds that followed him down the hall, tracking each step as the young boy turned the corner into the elevator bay.

A group of older passengers exited the elevator, cocktails in hand, laughing, and brushed past Owen. Paying no mind to the little boy all by himself.

A knock at the door pulled Reese's eyes up from the screen. Hendricks entered, gripping a small piece of purple fabric in her hands.

"May I?" Reese asked, extending his hand. Hendricks passed him the fabric, and he unfurled it for Mrs. Daley to examine.

It was a purple dress. A child-size medium, if he had to guess. The collar was stitched with white daisies, and the frock had two pockets down by the waist.

"Do you recognize this, Mrs. Daley?"

"No? Why would my son have a girl's dress?"

"Mmm. Had you seen him hanging around with any other children, maybe?"

"No, not today. He was with us all day. Just us and our other two kids."

Reese considered her responses. Kids on cruises had a habit of sneaking away somewhere for a bout of nervous kissing. But ten years old seemed a bit too young to fit that profile.

“Excuse me, ma’am,” Hendricks said to the anxious mother. “May I have a word with Officer Reese in private?”

“In private? Are you kidding? Anything you have to say regarding my son you can say to me!”

Hendricks looked to Reese for guidance.

“Just tell me, Tracy.”

“Sir, we found this dress on the sports deck . . . draped over one of the security cameras.”

“*Over* the camera?” Reese questioned. “I don’t follow.”

“Huh?” Mrs. Daley chimed in. “What does that mean?”

A covered security camera?

He rushed back to his computer. He sorted through the footage and found the cam feed for elevator six. There was Owen. Alone. He watched as the boy exited on the thirteenth floor and went through the sliding-glass doors and out onto the open-air deck.

Reese cycled through the feeds, finally pinpointing the camera for the basketball court.

“Aha! Here we go. He went to play basketball.” He angled the screen toward the two women.

They watched as Owen squeezed through the fence. The boy dribbled the ball and took a shot at the hoop in the strong wind. The ball hit the rim and bounced off. Reese skipped ahead in the footage. For two minutes, Owen practiced making baskets, missing every time.

And then . . . nothing. A faint, dark purple hue engulfed the entire screen.

For a moment, Reese thought the camera feed had cut out. But his eyes flicked down to the time stamp in the corner. Still ticking up.

22:57:13.

22:57:14.

22:57:15.

It had to be the dress. Hendricks was right. Someone purposefully placed it over the security camera.

Reese felt his eyes open wide. Hendricks noticed the shift in his demeanor.

"I don't understand what's happening," Mrs. Daley said. "Aren't there other cameras?"

"Give me one second, ma'am," Reese said.

From his memory of the predeparture walkthrough of the vessel, Reese knew there were two more cameras on the aft part of the thirteenth deck. He pulled up those camera feeds and scrubbed to the same time code.

One camera pointed toward the other end of the basketball court. He scanned the tape. The hoop sat undisturbed. No sign of Owen in frame or leaving the deck.

The other camera pointed toward the rock-climbing wall. Again. Nothing.

Damn it.

He scrolled through the other cameras on that end of the

ship, going down floor by floor on the off chance that any were pointed toward the deck above. Or perhaps Owen had climbed down a stairwell to a lower floor.

For the briefest of moments while scrubbing through the footage, something caught Reese's eye.

What the hell was that?

He backed up the footage a few seconds.

There.

It happened so fast that he wasn't sure exactly what he'd seen.

22:59:42.

A dark mass flew past the starboard camera on floor twelve. It rushed through the corner of the frame in a matter of milliseconds. But even through the darkness, there was no doubt something was there.

Something falling on the other side of the safety railing.

He backed up the time stamp and navigated to the camera feed on floor eleven.

Same thing. Falling at 22:59:42.

Reese tracked the falling object down floor by floor. He stopped at the gangway camera on the fourth floor. He leaned in toward the screen, squinting to closer examine the silhouette plunging down past each guardrail.

What is that?

Something small.

Something . . . *flailing.*

Reese shot up from his desk in a flash, grabbing his walkie-talkie.

"What is it? What's going on?" Mrs. Daley cried.

"Hendricks, stay here with her," he commanded, slipping his arms through his coat and bounding out the door.

"Yes, sir."

"Excuse me!" Mrs. Daley protested. "Officer Reese, what's happening? What's wrong?"

Reese's knees weren't what they used to be. The impact of each step sent twinges through his joints. From behind him, he could hear the music in the ballroom beginning to die down. The faint sound of "Closing Time" by Semisonic echoed through the halls of the ship.

He rounded the final flight of stairs. Punched his access code into the bridge's door and flung it open.

Captain DeForest stood with his back to Reese, looking out of the tinted glass window at the vast expanse of the dark ocean.

"Captain—" Reese wheezed. "You need to stop the boat right now!"

The bridge crew instantly turned toward him.

"We have a man overboard."

16

Powerful waves crashed against the side of the lifeboat. Tracy Hendricks and her team had shoved off from the *Atlantia* almost four hours ago, retracing the ship's path back to the approximate area where the child had presumably gone overboard.

She was under no illusion of their odds.

Two searchlights sliced through the frigid night air.

Different parts of the ocean revealed themselves every second as the boat rocked up and down on the swell. Unlike the relative steadiness of the massive cruise ship, this was nauseating.

"Shea, give me the readout on the water temperature gauge!" Hendricks shouted over the blasting wind.

"Fifty degrees Fahrenheit," he called out.

At that temperature, hypothermia could set in in as little as an hour.

And this boy had been in the water for more than seven . . .

With the weather deteriorating by the minute, and sea conditions worsening too, the boat listed wildly from side to side. Even wearing a thick life vest, Tracy shuddered at the thought of being in this water for even a second.

"*Owen!*" she yelled out across the water with a bullhorn, her voice hoarse from the past few hours of screaming. "*Owen!*"

She directed her flashlight's powerful beam into the places where the searchlights couldn't reach. Shouted again and again.

Nothing.

Not even a piece of trash floating on the surface.

Tracy directed the boat operator to complete another loop around the area. It was half past five in the morning, and those back on board the ship anxiously awaited word.

Thomas St. Clair—another security officer Tracy had hand-selected to join the search and rescue mission—made his way up to the bow and joined her on the bench. He motioned to the bullhorn, and Hendricks handed it over, appreciating the momentary relief. This futile back-and-forth had been their routine for hours now.

"*Owen!*" St. Clair bellowed out. "*Owen!* Can you hear us?"

Hendricks slumped down on the bench seat, her muscles exhausted from the past few hours of fighting the ocean and searching. She ran her hands through her hair and pressed hard against her temples. Sea spray crashed over the bow and continued to soak her and the crew. The skin on her face was tight and burning from the constant assault from the salt water.

"*Owen!*" St. Clair called out again into the darkness, swinging the searchlight from side to side. "*Owen!* Are you there?"

Hendricks looked over at the life rings propped up against the side of the boat, desperately wishing she had reason to use them. She considered the child's chances of survival.

Seven hours overboard. Fifty-degree water. Fifteen-foot waves. No life jacket . . .

Hendricks shook her head at the odds. Regardless, she had to try again. She stood back up and mustered all her strength to shout into the night.

"Owen! Owen, can you hear me? Owen!"

She waited, straining to listen for any possible signs of life. A distant cry for help.

Again, nothing.

Tracy slammed her fists down in frustration.

St. Clair lowered the bullhorn and rested his hand on her shoulder. "He's gone, Tracy. You know there's no way . . ."

She knew it.

They all knew it.

Just couldn't admit it to herself until they'd tried every

possible way to save the boy. They owed that to the poor kid's mother and father.

A nearly twenty-foot wave battered the side of the ship. Wind howled through the cabin. Tracy took one last look across the empty, lifeless sea and nodded.

"Shea, bring us back to the *Atlantia*. I'm calling it off."

Reese stood against the railing on the fourth deck, the lowest accessible point of the ship. He peered down into the brutal waves slamming against the side of the hull.

Since the search and rescue team had left on the lifeboat, he'd stationed himself here and waited, clutching his walkie-talkie close to his chest so that he could pick up the second they came within range. He prayed they found the kid. Alone, abandoned in the unforgiving ocean was no way to die.

A blinking beam of light appeared on the horizon. About three kilometers out, if he had to guess. It was the rescue boat heading back toward the *Atlantia*.

He depressed the Transmit button and prayed for the best. "Reese for Hendricks. Come in, Hendricks. Do you copy?"

The walkie-talkie rumbled with static.

"Hendricks? Anything?"

A voice struggled to break through the long distance.

"Neg—ative." The static faded, and Hendricks's voice became clearer. "Negative, Jake."

Reese lowered his head and took a deep breath in. It was too much for anyone to bear.

How the hell did this happen?

He knew the odds were astronomical but had held on to the slimmest of chances.

The boy was gone.

Reese headed back to the tenth floor to fulfill his horrible duty as the messenger.

He opened the door to the operations room.

Captain DeForest sat on the corner of the table, having spent the past few hours comforting the parents. He'd taken his hat off and placed it on the desk. The joyous gold trimming of the hat looked out of place in his bland environment. Especially in this moment.

Every member of the crew turned to Reese as he closed the door behind him. Owen's parents stared at him with a mix of hope and fear.

He slowly inhaled. "Mr. and Mrs. Daley, I am so sorry, bu—"

Before he could even finish, Mrs. Daley collapsed into her husband in a heap of screaming sobs. Mr. Daley's bottom lip quivered as he stroked his wife's back.

Reese noticed a pair of new faces in the corner of the room. It was Owen's siblings, a girl and a boy. A specialist from the medical team had come up to the operations room specifically for them. The two teenagers gazed ahead, clearly in shock. Blank. Emotionless. As if the news of this night wouldn't seep in until years down the road.

Captain DeForest tapped Reese on the shoulder.

"Accident or not," he whispered in a low, hushed tone, "I want you to find out what the hell is going on."

17

Steve snored like a lion. He had the itchy comforter wrapped around him and slept like he didn't have a care in the world.

Maria sat on the edge of the bed, her head in her hands, trying desperately to find the peace that had so easily lulled her fiancé to sleep. She'd managed to get a few winks of exhaustion-induced rest between each bout of tossing and turning. But when the engines cut off and the boat stopped moving at 2:00 a.m., that was it. Maria spent the rest of the night wide awake and preoccupied with what that could mean.

There was no use pretending. No amount of lying in bed was going to soothe her nerves.

The cheap alarm clock on the side table read out in bright red glowing numbers.

6:00 a.m. The sun would be rising soon.

Maria thought back to when they'd booked the trip. She looked around the extra bedroom, the place she and Steve had been so excited to use as a romantic escape from the kids. The thought of it seemed so petty now. Her mind couldn't have been further away.

She slunk out of the bedroom and closed the door slowly, making sure not to wake Chloe, whom Steve had delicately tucked in after she'd fallen asleep on the couch.

Maria cracked open the door to the smaller bedroom to get a peek of Christopher snoozing away on the twin-size bed. There he was, bathed beneath the blue nightlight she always plugged in for him, despite his assertions about being too old for such a childish device.

With the knowledge that her children were safe and sound, Maria threw on a comfortable sweatshirt and some Bermuda shorts before exiting the cabin.

A few early risers were already up and about. Maria nodded at the seniors who smiled her way, as if congratulating such a young woman for being up so early.

I just need somewhere to think.

Somewhere alone.

She made her way to the elevator bay in the middle of the ship. A map next to the elevator door gave a breakdown of what was on each deck. Her eyes scanned for anything secluded. In an instant, she'd found it.

The chapel.

She pulled out the folded-up paper schedule from her pocket. The next prayer service didn't start until 10:00 a.m.

Perfect.

The chapel was tucked away on the sixth floor, butted up against the back of the movie theater. It wasn't so much a chapel as a converted conference room. Sickly velveteen curtains hung in pleats around the walls. With only two rows of chairs, the entire thing was smaller than some of the deluxe staterooms where the upgraded passengers slept.

Keeping with the cruise ship's policy of religious equity, the room displayed no Christian iconography. Or any iconography, for that matter. Instead, in place of an altar, a set of two pillars topped with flower-filled urns flanked either side of a large abstract blue painting.

Maria opened the door and stopped dead in her tracks.

She wasn't alone.

A woman was crumpled in one of the chairs in the front row. She sobbed in quiet, rhythmic pulses. Heaving silently.

As if all the air in the room had already been swallowed up.

Maria turned slowly to leave, not wanting to startle the already deeply troubled woman. The door hinge groaned, giving her away. The woman whipped around.

"I'm so sorry, I didn't mean to interrupt," Maria said over her shoulder. She turned to leave.

"Wait . . . no," the woman choked out. "It's okay. Please.

Come in." The woman wiped her nose on her sleeve and brushed down the matted parts of her hair.

Maria considered just leaving anyway. The last thing she needed right now was to talk this woman through whatever alleged infidelity her husband had probably committed.

"Please," the woman said between sharp inhales. "I'm sorry . . . It's my . . . it's my son."

Maria turned back into the chapel and shut the door. Slid into the seat next to the woman. Placed a gentle hand on her back.

The woman burst into a sudden rush of tears.

"My name is Maria," she said gently. "Please, tell me about your son."

Maria had served as a grief counselor thousands of times. But always in a controlled office environment and with patients she had known for years. Though she wasn't a subscriber to the clichéd "Five Stages of Grief" approach, whatever pain this woman was experiencing was fresh. The wound had just opened.

"They can't . . . We can't . . . we can't find him."

"They can't find him? You mean he's missing? Here on the ship?"

The woman tucked her head into Maria's shoulder, crying softer than before.

"They think he went overboard . . . but they don't know

anything. They don't know anything. Maybe the wind, maybe . . . They don't know."

Oh no.

Maria swallowed hard, unable to fathom the grief this woman must be feeling. It was every parent's worst nightmare.

The woman looked up at her through desolate eyes.

A look she had seen somewhere before. But couldn't place exactly when.

"My God," Maria said. "I am so very sorry . . ."

"He loves sports . . . We should've known . . . He'd been asking to go to the basketball court all day. I should have let him go. Then . . . then he'd still be . . ."

Maria rubbed the woman's back as her voice faded mid-sentence.

"All they found on the court was a dress . . . a purple dress . . . but Owen . . . my boy is gone."

The woman exploded into tears at the sound of her own admission.

Maria involuntarily tightened her grip on the woman's back. "They found a dress?" she asked. "I'm sorry, you said they found a dress? What do you mean?"

The woman nodded. "Um . . . a little girl's dress. That's all they found on the basketball court."

"You didn't recognize the dress?"

"No. Why?"

Maria's heart began to race. She quickly stood to leave. "I am so very sorry, but I need to go."

The woman's head sank into her hands again, and she returned to sobbing.

As Maria raced out of the chapel, she remembered where she'd seen the look on that woman's face before.

Two years ago.

In the eyes of the bereaved parents inside the courtroom at Wyatt Butler's trial.

It's him.

He's here.

18

"Steve, wake up." Maria shook her fiancé with more force than she intended. "He's here, Steve. He's on the ship."

Steve grumbled and rolled onto his back. Reached over to the lamp on the bedside table and flicked it on.

Maria caught a glimpse of herself in the wave-shaped mirror that hung above the bedframe. She had dark rings around her eyes. Her T-shirt had creases. The warm glow from yesterday afternoon had long worn off. The lines in her face suddenly seemed more pronounced.

"Huh?" Steve replied groggily. "Who's on the ship?"

"Butler!"

"Shhh, sh, sh, sh!" Steve motioned toward where the twins slept.

Maria knew he'd been desperate to keep that name away from the twins as much as he could. And she appreciated his efforts. He kicked off the covers and eyed the alarm clock.

"Baby, it's 6:00 a.m. Did you even go to sleep last night?"

"You're not listening. Butler is on this ship!"

"What are you talking about?"

"I mean he's on this ship right now, and people are dying, Steve."

"No, Maria. He's not. This is a paranoid reaction to the rumors we've been—"

"Steve, this is real," Maria replied defiantly. "You must believe me. This is happening."

Steve took a deep breath and rubbed both his palms into his still-sleepy eyes. "Did you see him?" he asked.

"No, but—"

"So how do you know he's on the ship?"

Maria felt ready to tear her hair out. She stared into Steve's eyes.

There was that look. The look of incredulity.

"I just came from the chapel. The woman in there. Her son was playing basketball last night, alone. They think he might've gone overboard; that's why the ship was stopped for hours. And the only thing they found left behind at the basketball court was a dress. A little girl's dress."

"Okay . . . and?"

"*And?* What do you mean *and*?" Maria asked. "Steve, you're more obsessed with this case than I ever was. You of all people know this is precisely Butler's MO. These are his calling cards. The decapitated head with neck muscles tied in a ribbon? Leaving another child's clothes at the scene of a crime? He's calling out his next victim."

"Hold on. The scene of what crime? Let's say the mother was telling the truth—"

"She was, Steve. I know it."

As a psychologist, Maria had, over the years, developed an acute sense to tell when patients were lying. The woman in the chapel was not lying.

"Okay, so let's say she's telling the truth and her kid fell off the boat. That sounds to me like a terrible accident. As for the dress, I can't tell you how many items of clothes are already in the lost and found. I walked by the bin yesterday afternoon on the pool deck. There are dozens of things in there, from clothes to shoes to probably missing children too. There's no crime here, baby."

Maria ripped her hand out of his grip. "I know what I know, Steve."

"But you don't have any proof. Just hearsay."

"Just because you can't see it doesn't mean I'm wrong."

"Maria. Stop it. Seriously. You can't keep doing this. You're conflating details, rumors even, to piece together this theory. It makes no sense. Why would he be on this boat? Just by coincidence? I hate to say it, but honestly, you sound completely—"

"Stop." Maria cut him off before that accusatory word left his mouth.

Steve lowered his head and spoke softly. "Listen. Even if that little boy did go overboard—passengers fall overboard all the time. I'm telling you, cruise lines keep that kind of thing so tightly under wraps. But it happens. Think about it."

"Think about this instead: a man on board this ship was found decapitated. Then a child goes overboard. To think these events aren't related . . . that's what's crazy."

Steve shook his head. "Please, my love, you should get some rest. A good night's sleep will make you feel so much better. We'll go through this all again in a few hours, I promise."

He doesn't believe me.

Everything had been so perfect between the two of them. Maria felt a tear well up in the corner of her eye. Maybe it was from lack of sleep. Maybe Steve was right. Maybe what she was saying *was* crazy.

No. No. It can't be coincidental.

"If I'm right, more people are going to die," Maria maintained. "If I'm right, we might be in danger, Steve. *Christopher and Chloe* might be in danger."

Steve sighed and lay back on the bed. "Please, love, can't we just let this all go? I can't help you if you plan on making this crusade the entire trip."

"Fine, then stay with the kids and don't let them out of

your sight," Maria snapped. She walked over to the window and threw open the curtains. Morning streams of pink and orange sunlight engulfed the room.

"If you won't help me stop him, I'll do it alone."

19

Reese turned his key in the lock, sealing up his office door. He headed downstairs to his cabin for some much-needed physical and emotional rest.

It was almost eight in the morning, and the ship was moving again, most passengers likely oblivious to the fact that it had ever stopped to begin with. The boat stirred with morning activity. The smell of maple syrup and scrambled eggs wafted in down the hall from the buffet. A few of the ship's events coordinators were setting up a life-size game of bowling with inflatable pins. The sounds of shuffleboard clinks could be heard in the distance.

Hendricks had just radioed in. She was coming off a

nap since returning from the lifeboat. She'd be upstairs in a few minutes to take over for him while he got some sleep.

With his office on the tenth floor and his cabin on the seventh, Reese wanted to check on one last thing on his way down before collapsing into bed.

Room 817.

That entire section of the eighth floor had been cleared out. The guest services team had made quick work of relocating the passengers on that corridor to other empty cabins. The decapitated head had been put on ice and moved down to the morgue in the bowels of the ship. Reese patiently awaited the onboard medical examination team's final report. This would have to do in the meantime, until a proper analysis could be done when the ship reached Southampton. Their forensics capabilities on the ship were fairly limited.

He cast his mind back to earlier in the night. He'd scanned through the eighth floor's security footage with a fine-tooth comb, from the moment crewmembers had boarded the ship to the moment Pam Mayer and the maintenance worker discovered the head.

Nothing. No one had entered or exited that room the entire time. How someone had managed to get in and place a freshly decapitated head without detection was dumbfounding.

Maybe someone erased security footage tapes?

Who has access and knowledge of how to do that, besides Hendricks and me?

Reese left his office with this thought in mind.

Two of the morning security guards were just beginning their shift at the sectioned-off zone. He nodded at them as he made his way down the stairs. But something in front of the guards caught his eye.

A short woman in a light blue hoodie was giving the two officers an earful. She had a strange look in her eye.

Reese stepped closer to hear the conversation at the exact moment one of the guards gestured to him from down the hall.

"That's him right there," the officer said, pointing a finger at Reese and clearly trying to extricate himself from the conversation.

Goddamn it. So close.

The woman rushed up to him in a hurry, nearly knocking over a stack of room service trays piled up in the hallway. She extended her arm for a handshake. Reese reluctantly obliged.

"Hi, hi. I'm Maria Fontana, staying in cabin 925. Can I get a word with you real quickly? It's extremely important."

"Is it an emergency, Ms. Fontana?" Reese replied, desperately hoping the answer was no.

"Yes, it is."

"If it's an emergency, can you tell me now, please?"

"I'd really rather speak to you behind closed doors. It won't take long, I promise."

Through the haze of his sleep-deprived brain, Reese's training kicked back in. Suspecting domestic violence, he leaned in close to her and spoke in a low tone.

"Ms. Fontana, has someone on board hurt you? I'm here to help, if—"

"No, no, I'm all right. I just have some information I think you might want to hear."

Reese looked back down the stairs. His cabin—and his bed—were directly beneath his feet one floor below. He heaved a sigh and turned back toward the ascending staircase.

"Follow me, Ms. Fontana."

Reese unlocked the door to his office and offered the woman a seat.

"I'm sorry if I'm interrupting anything, Officer Reese," Maria said.

"Please, call me Jake. And no, I was just headed down to my cabin to get some rest."

"A sleepless night, I imagine."

"Yes, well, as I'm sure you can understand, we've been very busy. Keeping several thousand people safe is a demanding task."

"But we aren't safe, are we?" Maria asked.

Reese straightened in his chair. "I'm sorry?"

"Excuse me, I apologize. I didn't get much sleep last night either. Let me explain myself." Maria took a deep breath, sat up straight, and continued, "I'm sure you're familiar with Wyatt Butler? The serial killer case a few years ago?"

Reese thought for a moment. "Wyatt Butler? He was that accused child murderer from New York, if I remember correctly. They let him go, right?"

"Yes, they did. Believe me when I say I know this sounds crazy, but I think Butler might be on this ship."

Reese arched an eyebrow. "Wyatt Butler?"

"And if not him, then maybe a copycat. Someone who's using Butler's playbook."

Great. Now a true-crime fanatic in my office.

Reese let out a long, deep sigh. "Hold on, back up for a second. What makes you think Butler is here?"

"I believe he might be responsible for the missing child. The boy from the basketball court."

"Missing child?"

"Yes," Maria replied. "I ran into his mother earlier this morning in the chapel. We spoke for a few minutes. Poor family."

Reese shook his head. "I'm sorry, Ms. Fontana, but—"

"She said your people found a little girl's dress at the scene," Maria said, cutting him off. "When I heard that, I knew it had to be him. It's too much to be a coincidence. And the decapitated head on the eighth floor? With the neck muscles meticulously tied in a ribbon?"

"Where did you hear *that*?"

"It doesn't matter where."

The two locked eyes across the desk. He was impressed by her tenacity. And seemingly endless access to privileged information.

"My point is," she added, "there's only one person who has a habit of killing people like that. And it's Wyatt Butler."

Reese stared at Maria for a lingering moment, studying her face for ulterior motives or deceit.

She's taking herself seriously.

Which means she's either a fanatic or nutjob.

"Two problems, Ms. Fontana. That guy Butler was found not guilty. So if he is on this boat, so be it. Second, I never heard any mention of him tying veins into ribbons, or anything like what you mentioned."

He made sure he was careful not to admit that anything this woman had heard on board the ship was accurate. For a start, he had no idea how the rumors had gotten out. Second, the speed that they'd spread had defied belief.

"No, you wouldn't have heard those kinds of details," Maria replied. "They hid that information from the media. But I assure you, the crime scene photos they showed us in the courtroom were far more graphic and were exactly the same as—"

"Hold on a second," Reese stopped her. "In the courtroom? What's your connection here?"

"Officer Reese, I was one of the jurors."

"You're kidding me." *Okay, now I'm sure she's crazy.*

"Listen, I know how far-fetched all of this must sound. Please. Just run a search for his name on the passenger manifest. I'm sure you have the ability to right there—"

"You know I can't do that with you in the room, Ms. Fontana. It's a breach of passenger privacy."

"Then do it when I leave. Or at least run a search for men on board traveling alone. It's very possible he's changed his identity."

Reese wiped a bead of sweat from his forehead. The anxiety dripping off this woman had started to seep into him. He leaned back in his chair, taking in the situation.

"This man. Butler." Maria leaned forward in her chair. "He's obsessive-compulsive. Driven by ego. He's violent. It's very likely he suffers from antisocial personality disorder. Exhibits a total lack of empathy for others. The result is a kind of sociopathic cocktail. He's a deadly combination."

Reese's eyes widened. The way she spoke reminded him of the countless behavioral experts the Miami Criminal Division brought in to testify in their most unusual of cases. All those experts had known their shit, but Maria instantly came across as a superior version of them.

"So?" she said.

"What are you, ex–law enforcement or something? A profiler?"

"Not quite. I'm the head of the Psychology Department at Columbia University. And I know more about this case than possibly anyone alive."

An academic.

"Ms. Fontana, you may be a firsthand witness to the Butler case. But as far as I'm concerned, the Butler case is not *my* case. What hard evidence do you have that he's even on this ship?"

"None, yet," she admitted. "But . . . the neck. The missing child. The dress. All of it fits his MO to a tee. His compulsions are uncontrollable."

"You seem to have him pretty well diagnosed. Was he a patient of yours too?" Reese asked.

"I studied him in that courtroom for weeks. I can safely say that my assessment is on target, if not clinically accurate."

Well, she's certainly confident in her own abilities.

"I've been doing this for a long time, Jake," Maria said sternly.

"So have I, Columbia. But okay, I'll play ball. Let's say you're right. Now why on earth would he be on this ship in the first place?"

"He must know I'm on board with my family. That's the only thing I can figure."

Reese had to hide the incredulous expression threatening to take over his face.

Maria pressed on. "His fate was in my hands in the trial. And now, he feels like the shoe is on the other foot. Maybe he's here to taunt me. I'm not certain."

"How would he even know that you'd be on this ship?"

"That . . ." Maria broke her intense eye contact for just a moment. "I'm not certain of. But it's not hard to imagine ways of finding it out. We've had this trip booked for a while."

"Well, Ms. Fontana. Here's why I think what you've got doesn't add up. Butler was an alleged child killer. The man who lost his life was an adult. Not only that, but there is no evidence that the child falling overboard was anything more than an accident. I think what you've got is a classic case of forcing soft evidence to fit your carefully constructed theory."

"But what about the dress? Butler placed stolen children's clothing at the crime scene as a kind of signal, a calling card for who his next victim would be."

"Ms. Fontana, do you know how many articles of lost clothing are on board this ship?"

Reese rubbed his weary eyes and looked out the window at the sunlight sparkling brilliantly off the waves. "Listen, what we've got on our hands is one incident and one accident.

There's nothing to suggest that the two are related. And though the incident might be unusual, it's my job to keep this ship in order. Whatever personal history you might have is not my concern at the moment."

"Please. You have to believe me. Just look into it. If I'm right, everyone on this ship might be in danger. And the problems you've got on your hands will only get worse."

"If I look into it, do you promise to keep calm out there with the other passengers? The last thing I need right now is more hearsay."

She gritted her teeth at the slight but looked up at him with understanding eyes. "You have my word."

They both stood and shook hands. She gave him a firm nod, spun away, and headed out.

Finally alone, Reese looked around the office he'd been so desperate to escape. He sat back down and flipped open a manila folder on his desk. Pulled out crime scene images from the eighth floor.

There was the head. Neck viscera tied into a neat bow at the base.

He considered the things Maria had said.

The head of the Psychology Department at Columbia . . . well, she can't be a complete crackpot.

He dug through the file and pulled out a plastic bag. Inside, the sheet of paper Hendricks had taken out of the typewriter read as clear as day.

`If the judicial system can't stop him, who will?`

The quote swirled in Reese's head.

Could the "him" *really be Butler? Or someone pretending to be Butler?*

He swiveled his chair over to the desktop computer. The entire office had internet access hardwired in for occasions just like this one. He pulled up Google and typed in the cryptic quote from the paper into the search bar, adding *Wyatt Butler* to the end of the phrase.

Within an instant, tens of thousands of hits flashed up on the screen.

There.

The first search result was a link to a bookseller's website, the page entitled: *Wyatt Butler: The Ultimate Truth* by Jeremy Finch.

Reese clicked on the URL. It was a link to buy some tell-all crime book written about the case. He hit control-F and searched for the quote on the page. It popped up in the free excerpt from the book.

Highlighted in yellow, the quote was the last sentence of the book's introduction.

He scrolled down.

What the hell?

Reese almost fell backward out of his chair.

Near the bottom of the page, a proud photo of the author sat in gleaming color next to his bolded name.

Jeremy Finch.

But Reese recognized him immediately: the man whose decapitated head was currently sitting in the ship's morgue.

20

Chloe and Christopher sat slumped on the couch, clacking their checker pieces across the game board unenthusiastically. The cabin's living room was starting to feel cramped.

Steve sat in the armchair beside them and lazily flipped through the activity schedule, searching for anything he thought might get Maria's mind off this Butler nonsense.

Bingo . . . nope.

Zumba class . . . nope.

A beer pong tournament . . . definitely not.

There was still six days to go on the ship, and Maria's nightmarish memories of the trial had threatened to spoil them all. Still threatened to spoil *them.*

The cabin door flew open with a bang. Steve jumped. The

kids' head snapped in the direction of the entrance. Maria hustled into the room, appearing flustered.

"Mom!" Chloe said.

"Agh! You didn't bring back breakfast?" Christopher moaned.

Maria leaned down and gave each of the kids a quick peck on the head. "Sorry, guys. We'll get you some food soon, I promise."

She hurried into the smaller bedroom with the twin beds. Steve followed her in and closed the door behind him.

"Maria. Where have you been?"

She didn't answer. Instead, she opened the dresser where they'd unpacked the twins' clothes and dug through the folded piles.

"Maria? Maria?" Steve asked.

She looked up at him out of the corner of her eye. "I met with the head of ship security. Told him everything. About Butler, about the crime scene, the dress. Everything. He's going to look into it all, but I'm not sure how much he believes me yet."

"Hold on, slow down, slow down," Steve replied. "Take a deep breath, baby."

"There's no time." She pulled away back toward the dresser and opened the middle drawer.

"Maria," Steve pleaded. "Let me help you. What are you looking for?"

"I'm going through Chloe's clothes."

"Why?"

"I'm making sure all of her dresses are here."

"Jesus, Maria." Steve shook his head. "Okay. Here, let me help too. Let's check together."

One by one, they counted each outfit they'd packed for the kids. Twelve sets of shirts, eight sets of shorts, twenty-four pairs of socks, ten bathing suits, and four dresses for Chloe.

Everything was there.

"Thank God," Maria said.

"There. See? Everything's fine."

She turned to him. "I'm going back out, just for a little bit. Don't let the kids out of your sight for a second."

"Wait, please. Just wait a second! Maria, let's talk about this."

"I'll go quickly. If I don't find him, I'll come back and we can get breakfast with the kids."

"Find who?" Steve replied in shock. "You're going out there looking for *Butler*? You can't be—"

"It's either Butler or there's a copycat on this boat. Security doesn't even know what they're looking for. I do."

"Maria. Seriously? Have you lost your mind?"

"I promise, just one lap of the ship and I'll come right back." Maria headed out into the living room. Steve trailed behind her, struggling to keep up.

"Okay, listen up, you two," Maria said to the kids. "I want

you to stay here with Steve, you understand? Play some games for a little bit, then shower up and I'll be back."

Chloe rolled her eyes. "Okay, Mom. We got it."

"Look at me," Maria commanded. "Promise me you will not leave Steve's side."

"Okay! We won't!" Christopher said.

"And I want you all here safe and sound when I get back."

Before Steve had a chance to protest, she'd already tightened her sandals and slammed the door behind her.

He stood there for a moment, blankly staring at the emergency exit instructions posted below the peephole. His fiancée had gone mad, and there was seemingly nothing he could do to stop it. The twins had already gone back to their game of checkers.

Steve let out a resigned sigh. This was all happening again, the paranoia, the fear. The same things that crippled their relationship for months after the trial.

For a long time, Maria had become a recluse, shying away from going out in public. And in the times that Steve had actually coaxed her out of the house, she exhibited classic paranoia. Felt people were always watching her, or following the family.

It took months to build up to the trip.

Maybe we went on this vacation too soon . . .

Something needs to be done.

She's spiraling again.

He lifted the grimy TV remote control off the coffee table and turned on the tiny TV screen. The default Cruising on Board channel flickered to life.

Steve hit the button until he found the Disney Channel. The sounds of *Descendants* filled the room, catching the twins' immediate attention. They dropped the game pieces and turned to watch.

"My favorite show!" Chloe excitedly shouted.

The twins were rapidly enchanted.

Nothing would distract them from the television.

Slowly, Steve backed away into his bedroom. He turned and looked at the door to exit the cabin.

Maria weaved in and out of the crowded buffet line, turning back to check every face she passed. If Butler was on board, she wondered if she'd even recognize him. And what if this was the work of a copycat? What then?

Regardless, each person she passed seemed alien to her. Somehow off. Artificial.

The smell of the breakfast sausages piled up in the aluminum serving trays made her nauseous, but she was determined to get a good look at as many people as possible. She'd come at the perfect time of day. Nearly everyone on the ship piled Belgian waffles and bacon onto their plates.

When she'd finished checking the faces in line, she moved on to the passengers already seated in the dining hall.

There were hundreds of families at hundreds of tables. They could mostly be counted out, since Butler operated as a lone wolf. She circled around each table like a vulture. She eyed everyone else with critical eyes, looking for the slightest suspicion or odd behavior.

There!

Near the juice bar, a man sat at a table alone. From across the room, he looked like a good fit for Butler. Midforties. Lean build. Dark sunglasses. Maria slunk behind a column and watched him pick at a pile of wet scrambled eggs. She braced herself on the concrete pillar, gathering the courage to march and confront him. Expose him to the rest of the passengers.

Just as Maria pushed off toward him, a woman joined the man at the table and gave him a kiss on the lips. Another couple set down their plates too, laughing about how long the make-your-own-omelet line had taken. Maria slipped back behind the column.

Damn it. Not him.

She tried to remember the last time she'd eaten. Yesterday morning, maybe?

Grabbing a banana can't hurt.

She nonchalantly circled back around the salad bar and reached for a fruit bowl.

Then froze.

Shit.

Through the sneeze guards, across the buffet, the strange

man stood directly opposite. The one she'd seen peering down to the pool deck in a heavy sweater. He caught her eye for a brief moment.

Maria quickly grabbed an apple and melted back into the herd of passengers, praying he hadn't noticed her. She circled the hot plate and caught a sight of him again.

He had a thick beard that obscured the outline of his jaw. A worn hat with the brim pulled down and bulky, ill-fitting clothes—like yesterday. Perhaps trying to conceal a thinner profile within. He looked uncomfortable in his own skin. Out of place.

Maria followed him. He dumped his dirty tray off on the conveyor belt and exited the buffet. Ambled down the hallway at a slow speed. She kept a safe distance. There were a handful of passengers between them, all making their way back to their cabins to change into bathing suits for the day.

The man glanced back over his shoulder.

Maria ducked behind a taller woman and kept in line with her, step for step. After a few seconds, she peeked back out.

The man had disappeared.

Damn!

Maria picked up speed. She reached a cross in the hallways. The spa to her left. The upper level of the theater in front of her. A staircase to her right. She bounded down the stairs, entering the first floor of passenger cabins.

No sign of him.

She started down one of the long corridors of staterooms. Not a single person in sight.

Where the hell did he go?

If he'd gone into a room, she had no chance of catching him. She doubled back to leave the hall.

There! Got him!

The man had reappeared heading down toward the theater.

Suddenly, something crashed against her hip.

A laundry cart being pushed out of a stateroom.

"Oh, I'm so sorry, ma'am!" the attendant cried out from inside the cabin.

Searing pain shot through Maria's pelvis. She clutched her side, waved off the attendant, and limped forward.

She had to keep moving. Take this chance to discover his identity in case it was her last.

The man rounded a corner and ducked beneath a neon sign. He headed into a new area of the ship, packed with slot machines and assorted table games. Maria, now hobbling, winced as she struggled to keep up.

The casino stank of cigarettes, even at this time in the morning. It was the only place on the ship where smoking inside was permitted. She ducked behind the first slot machine and observed her target. The man went up to the bar, passed off his key card, and accepted a plastic cup from the bartender.

Going for a beer? At nine in the morning?

Maria tried to recall if the prosecution had mentioned

anything about Butler's drinking habits during the trial, but nothing came to mind.

The man saddled up in front of one of the dozens of slot machines and slid his key card into the port. For the next ten minutes, she watched him intently as he gambled, yanking the lever over and over again, occasionally taking sips of his beer and puffs of his cigarette.

"Ma'am? Would you like to join in on this game of poker?"

Maria glanced back at the dealer who'd called out to her. "No, I'm all right. Thank you." She looked back to the row of slot machines.

He was gone.

Maria felt a finger tap twice on her shoulder. She whipped around.

The bearded man stood inches from her face. Startled, she stumbled back a step.

"If I didn't know any better, I'd say you're following me."

The smell of tar and cheap beer blasted in her face. A faint smell of body odor crept into her nostrils. The man had a slight midwestern twinge to his voice, vastly different from the Brooklyn cadence Butler had back in the courtroom.

Maria stared at every inch of his face, taking in each freckle. Each wrinkle. Desperately trying to recall Butler's features from her memory.

Same height. Same build. Same eye color, hair color.

His face looks different, but could he be?

"Now why would that be?" the man continued. "And you're the same lady who shot me a nasty look on the pool deck yesterday. So what's your problem?"

Maria took in every detail. The slant of his shoulders. His posture. She looked down at the cup of beer in his hand. Curled between his index and middle finger, his key card was tucked into his palm. If she could just get a look at it, she'd have his name.

"Are you listening to me?"

The man shook his head and turned to walk away.

"Who are you?" she finally asked, trying to hide the tremble in her voice.

The man slowly turned back to face her. "I beg your pardon? Who are *you*?"

"Where's your family? How about your friends?" Maria said. "You're traveling alone, aren't you? Why?"

"That's none of your damn business, lady!"

One of the casino attendants, a blackjack dealer at a nearby table, noticed the commotion and came over to the two people arguing in the middle of the floor. "Is he bothering you, ma'am?" the dealer asked, instinctively taking Maria's side.

"Am I bothering *her*?" the man shouted. "She's the one bothering me!"

"Why won't you just tell me your name?" Maria fired back.

"Listen, lady. I don't know what kind of game you're playing. But I don't want any part of it."

He turned to walk away.

Without thinking, Maria reached for the key card in his hand. The man yanked his arm away, knocking the plastic cup out of his other hand and onto the floor. Beer splashed in every direction, dousing both their clothes in a torrent of foam.

"Stay the hell away from me!"

The man backed away from Maria and hurried out of the casino, angry.

"Get back here!" Maria shouted. But he was gone.

"Ma'am, do you need help of some kind?" the dealer said gently. "Can I call someone?"

Maria ignored the question, brushed the beer off her sweatshirt, and headed out toward the same exit, following the best—and only—lead she had.

21

There she is.

Unsure what she is searching for . . .

The man stared intently as Maria left the casino, her clothes still dripping with beer. He'd seen everything. Maria hypnotically focused on the slot machines. The confrontation with that bearded passenger. And even now, he watched as she regained her composure outside the gift shop by the casino's exit. He'd followed her every step of the way, keeping his eyes trained on her from the outer limits of his vision.

He'd took up his station by the tacky, duty-free jewelry store, pretending to be perusing the clearly blemished diamonds. A stack of bracelet boxes on top of the plexiglass display case sat misaligned.

Instinctually, he leaned over the counter and nudged each angled box into place, creating a perfect little cardboard tower.

There.

"Um, excuse me, sir? Please don't touch anything," the mousey girl behind the counter asked with an edge to her voice. "If you'd like to examine any of the merchandise, please just ask me and I'll—"

The man raised his index finger up to his lips, as if to shush the clerk. Taken aback, she stopped speaking.

He turned and exited the store, following closely behind Maria as she marched down the hallway, completely oblivious to his presence.

He sauntered with his hands in his pockets. Examined every deep black curl of her hair. It spilled down her back like a black waterfall. Clean and bouncy.

Even with her short stature, she maneuvered quickly. Haphazardly. Cutting through the slow, ambling herd of degenerates like a razor-sharp knife. Brushing shoulders with slower-moving passengers.

Her moves were chaotic. Unfocused.

It bothered him.

Maria glanced over her shoulder. He smoothly ducked behind one of the tall sunglasses display cases that lined this retail portion of the ship. He'd already anticipated a fast move to avoid the searching glare of her wild eyes.

She made a right turn and carried on down the stairs. The man stepped back out into view and picked up speed.

The staircase bustled with smiling passengers, their filthy sandals slapping against the even filthier floor. He guessed barely any of them had noticed the ship's full engine stop last night. Though he'd heard a few whispers at breakfast. Witnesses who could've sworn they'd seen a lifeboat deployed in the middle of the night.

But by now, the rumors had mostly fizzled away.

Oblivious. Idiots.

He felt sick to even be among them like this. His skin crawled with each inch of cheap Hawaiian-printed linen and terry cloth cover-up that brushed by his arms. The thought of their naked bodies made his stomach churn even more. Sweating. Touching. Existing.

Mercifully, upon reaching the ninth floor, Maria took a sharp turn around the corner toward the various staterooms. The man followed a few seconds behind, taking a gasp of air once he was free of the pedestrian stink.

The long corridors with passenger cabins were narrow and thin. Zero sunlight. Claustrophobic. Maria slowed a bit, maybe even adding a touch of a limp to her walk as she gripped her hip, seemingly in pain.

He looked backward down the other end of the hall. No one.

It's just the two of us.

Adrenaline suddenly surged through his body.

If she turned around now, there was no place to hide.

She'd know she'd been followed.

She'd see him.

His head swooned from the rush.

He picked up his pace. Inhaling through his nose to stay silent. He got close enough to smell the salt of the sweat that had dried against her hairline.

His knuckles curled into his palms, digging the white tips of his nails into his skin, nearly drawing his own blood.

Just as he was about to reach her, he made an abrupt turn into a stairwell and ascended back up to the twelfth deck.

As much as he would have liked . . .

Her turn will have to wait.

The Kids' Zone on the twelfth floor was colorful and obnoxiously loud. An air hockey table in the center of the room provided the rhythmic clacking soundtrack. Two acne-ridden boys shot at virtual deer with cheap plastic rifles. The row of car-racing games was especially busy, each seat occupied by screaming tweens.

A circle of disinterested parents hovered outside the arcade, chatting about the surprisingly good dance show they'd seen in the main theater the night before. Ignoring their awful children.

A huddle of kids by the claw machine argued over who should get the next try. They sent an ambassador to beg for more game tokens from the parents out front. One young boy triumphantly clung to the cheap stuffed dinosaur toy he'd already pulled from the machine as a kind of trophy over the other kids. As if he were somehow blessed or bound for greatness in his life. He pulled it away from his grabby little sister.

The man watched from nearby, sitting on a bench outside of the ship's spa. Through the glass, he could see every disgusting act inside the arcade.

All the chaos.

It was unbearable to watch. His head began to pound from an impending migraine. The noise had to be stopped.

Within seconds, he found what he'd been looking for.

There she is . . .

The little girl had a short, bob hairstyle and bangs that hung just above her eyebrows. The lines were sharp. The cuts were precise. Her smile was speckled with braces. Her nose sloped up at the end. She was tall for her age. Developed. Even from here, the man could sense the teen boys eyeing her with desire.

She and her friends waited in line for the Skee-Ball machine.

It's a shame.

She probably looked nice in that purple dress.

22

Reese's chance to get some sleep had snowballed into a frantic deep dive on Wyatt Butler—and the wickedly evil crimes he'd allegedly committed. After hours of scouring the internet, making calls to old cop buddies, and reviewing case files, Reese realized Maria Fontana was certainly right about a few things.

The similarities between the decapitated head in the cabin and the bodies of Butler's supposed victims were too great to be ignored.

This author, Jeremy Finch, was a loner. A reclusive blogger who'd spent most of his life doing the same thing Reese found himself doing right now: chasing shadows on the internet.

Estranged from his family and unmarried, it was unlikely that anyone knew this guy was even missing. Reese imagined that it would be Finch's publishing agent that would need to identify him when they reached England.

With an especially brutal murder like this, the motive was almost always personal. But with no jilted ex-lovers or any major financial debts, the pool of candidates narrowed further.

That said, the fact that Fontana, the secondary villain of Finch's tell-all book, was even on this boat to begin with felt like too much of a coincidence.

And then there was Maria's press conference almost a year ago. A public admission that she'd voted on behalf of Butler's innocence. That she was the one who'd set him free. That fact alone injected an entirely different context to the conversation they'd had earlier that morning.

Why all of a sudden is she crying wolf on Butler now?

What changed her mind?

This misshapen new layer of information made Reese think something more sinister may be brewing.

What if she and Butler had been in on it the entire time? What if she was planted on the jury purposefully? To set him free?

It seemed far-fetched.

Though her being on this cruise, along with the decapitated head of the author who trash-talked her in his book, also seemed far-fetched. But it was true.

By the time he'd stumbled onto the viral video of Fontana accosting Finch at the bookstore, a theory had started to take root in his mind.

The latch on the door clicked open. Hendricks took one step into the room and gave Reese a look of disappointment.

"Please don't tell me you've been here this whole time, Jake," Hendricks said, unclipping her gun from her waist and setting it down in the safe. "It's getting tense outside."

"I've got something here, Tracy. I need your help figuring out how it all ties together."

"What good will you be if you fall asleep the second we have to chase down some jerk?" Hendricks folded her arms across her chest. "Seriously. You need to get some rest."

"I will. But you *need* to see this."

Detail by detail, Reese filled her in on his encounter with Maria Fontana. He explained her connection to the case and the eerie similarities between the Finch crime scene and the evidence from Butler's trial. He saved Maria's theory for last: the thing that had been keeping him up all night.

"I'm telling you, this woman. Fontana. She's certain that Butler's on the *Atlantia*."

"Well . . . is he?"

"See, that's where I'm not sure. I already went through the manifest. There's no one named Wyatt Butler on this ship. In passengers or crew."

"He could've changed his name after the trial. I certainly would have, if I were him."

"Right. So I searched for anyone on board traveling completely alone that fit his profile. White male. Tall. Midforties."

"And?"

"Well, there is one. Named . . ."

Reese shuffled through the mess of papers on his desk, looking for the right printout. "Here it is. *Colin P. Fisher.* But he's got a strong alibi. Runs a pest control business over in New Jersey. He's been living out there for the last fifteen years. Records show that he was doing exterminations and house visits during the entirety of the Butler trial."

"So it's not him."

"Well . . . who's to say Butler didn't kill that Fisher guy and take his identity, to get on the boat undetected?"

"You sure you're okay?" Hendricks made her way to the coffee machine to pour them both a strong cup. She dropped sugar in both and returned to the desk. "Listen to yourself, Jake. You're starting to sound like one of those wacky conspiracy theory people."

"I'm good."

"You're sure?"

"I'm fine," Reese said sternly, half trying to convince himself too. "I just think at this point, it's probably worth paying this Mr. Fisher a visit."

Hendricks gave a dismissive shake of her head.

Something told Reese that she wanted all of this to be resolved just as badly as he did.

In the easiest and safest way possible.

"We might as well," she finally agreed.

Reese couldn't help but grin.

"But let's go into this smart," Hendricks said. "Here's what we know for sure. We have one crime scene on board. As far as we know, the kid that fell overboard could still have been an accident."

"So, now for the obvious question. Who on board this ship has the most motive to murder the journalist that ruined their lives?"

He and Hendricks shared a knowing look.

She nodded. "I'd say Maria Fontana and her fiancé are our number-one suspects."

23

The ship rocked imperceptibly beneath Steve's feet. Only the sound of the creaking screw in the bedroom window broke the silence in the stateroom. Chloe and Christopher were in the smaller bedroom, taking an afternoon nap.

He stood over the coffee table in the living room and picked up the next shirt. The twins' clothes were still in disarray from Maria's mad dash through the cabin. He'd brought the unorganized pile of T-shirts and bathing suits out to the main room so he could reorganize the mess his fiancée had left in her wake.

Steve lifted a pair of Christopher's shorts off the couch—a maroon color with cargo pockets on either side. He snapped a loose thread off one of the belt loops and folded the pair in half.

He folded again.

Then unfolded the same pair.

Then folded it back.

Then unfolded.

Again and again.

Methodically.

Precisely.

He stared toward the balcony, idly watching as the waves flowed.

He folded the shorts again.

Then unfolded.

A loud knock at the cabin door snapped him out of his daze. Steve dropped the shorts and rushed over to the peephole.

Two figures, dressed head to toe in navy-blue uniforms, loomed in the hallway. A man and a woman. Tall. Stern. Serious. Definitely official.

Steve depressed the handle and cracked the door. "Hi, can I help you?"

"Steve Brannagan?" the man asked. "I hope we're not interrupting anything."

Steve glanced down to the holstered pistol on the man's hip.

"I'm Jake Reese," the man continued. "Head of security for the *Atlantia*. And this is my second-in-command, Officer Tracy Hendricks. Do you mind if we come in and ask you a few questions? Just a quick chat."

Head of security? Oh no.

Steve knew he had no choice. He swung the door open. "Is this about Maria? Is she all right? Did she do something?"

"Why do you think she did something, Mr. Brannagan?" Reese asked. "She's not in there with you?"

"No, she's not here. She's been . . . a little on edge lately. I'm not sure where she's at right now."

"You're not certain where your fiancée is?"

"Yes, that's right. She ran out pretty quickly earlier."

The security officers stood unmoved by the door. Emotionless. Steve could feel their eyes judging his every word and action.

"You're who she met with this morning?" Steve wondered aloud. "Ship security?"

Reese nodded. "Yes. May we come in, please?"

"Oh yes, sorry. Please." Steve stepped to the side and allowed the two officers into the living room. "Whatever you need, Officers."

He rushed over to the couch and grabbed the folded clothes so they could take a seat. Steve rapidly scanned the room for anything else out of place. After a moment, he had to say something to break the awkward silence.

"Would you like anything?" Steve asked. "How about some coffee?"

"I don't think your cabin has a coffee maker, Mr. Brannagan," Hendricks replied.

"Right, right. Sorry. I don't really know how to do this. Feels like having guests at home. But different."

Steve collapsed down in the small armchair. He motioned his head toward the smaller bedroom's door. "We'll have to keep the volume down. The kids are sleeping in there."

"Kids. Your children?" Reese asked.

"No, Maria's. From her first marriage. They'll officially be my stepkids after our wedding."

Reese nodded. "I see."

"Is everything all right?" Steve asked. "I know Maria's been saying some very concerning things, but she's just going through a little paranoia spell."

"Well, that's why we're here. You and Maria. How long have the two of you been together?"

"We met just after the trial, so . . . almost two years, I wanna say."

"Did Maria ever discuss the Butler trial with you? Ever tell you about any of the case details?" Hendricks chimed in.

"Well, not really, no. The things she saw in that courtroom were really disturbing. I tried to get her to open up about it, but she keeps it pretty private." Steve leaned forward in his chair and gave the security guards a wry smile. "To be honest with you, I know everything about Wyatt Butler and the case anyway. I know it's dark, but I find the character study incredibly fascinating. I dabble in part-time acting at home."

"You find it fascinating," Reese said rhetorically. "This

might sound strange, but do you believe Maria has had any contact with Butler since the trial?"

"With Butler? No, of course not!" Steve's voice grew a little too loud. His eyes shot over to the bedroom door, hoping he hadn't woken up the twins. He brought his volume back down to a whisper. "Why would she be talking to Butler?"

"Then do you know why she might believe Butler is on board the ship?"

"It's all the rumors. She heard some pretty ugly things going around the ship. Is it true you found a decapitated head?"

The two officers stared back.

No response.

They're here to question me. Not the other way around.

"Well, regardless of what you found," Steve said, "she's convinced it was him. She also thinks Butler was involved with the kid that went overboard. But I assured her that this kind of stuff happens on cruises all the time, right? I mean, you guys would know better than I would. But that's what Google says, so . . ."

Hendricks and Reese stared back at him with stone-cold expressions. Unreadable. Annoying. Like they'd stay here all night, acting like cynical statues, making him feel awkward.

"So, anything else you want to know?" Steve asked.

"Just one more question. What do you know about Jeremy Finch?"

"The author? If you can even call him that. What about him?"

"Did either you or your fiancée know him personally?" Hendricks asked.

"Hell no. Only met him once. But he's a real piece of work. A nasty son of a bitch." Steve made a mock sign of the cross. "Pardon my language. He's responsible for a lot of the shit that's gone on in our lives the past year."

The room went quiet again. The two officers glanced at each other, like they knew exactly what each other was thinking, despite the lack of clarity in their questions.

Hendricks finally stood from the couch. "Well, Mr. Brannagan. I think we've got enough information for now. We're sorry for the intrusion."

Steve sprang from the armchair. "Oh, no worries at all. I'd love to help out in any way I can. And I'm sorry if Maria has been pestering you. I know you're just trying to do your jobs. She stumbled into some real bad luck getting picked for that trial."

"Well, we've all got to do our civic duty."

As they moved toward the door, both peered into the open bathroom.

They're looking for something.

Just before the two officers walked out, Reese turned back toward the living room. "Thank you for your time, Mr. Brannagan," he said. "I hope you and the kids enjoy the rest of your voyage. If you need something or would like to tell us anything else, my office is on the tenth floor."

"Thank you, I'll keep that in mind."

He shut the door behind Reese and Hendricks, plunging the stateroom back into silence.

Steve shook his head, rattled and confused by the entire encounter. He needed to calm down. Do something therapeutic. He returned to the pile of clothes on the floor and picked up the same pair of shorts. Christopher's.

He examined them in his hands.

And folded them in half.

24

Reese and Hendricks strode along the corridor, away from cabin 925.

"Well, that was weird as hell," Hendricks said once they were out of earshot.

"Agreed. Let's keep an eye on him. I want camera feeds tracking his movements on the ship. And the same goes for Ms. Fontana too."

On the surface, Steve Brannagan seemed like a run-of-the-mill geek. While his admitted obsession with the Butler case was a clear red flag, his concern about his fiancée's mental well-being seemed sincere. Sneaking a decapitated head on board seemed a little too hard-core for the character display he'd put on today.

But then again, even the gentlest souls are capable of evil.

We can't rule anything out.

Or anyone.

The two made their way down the ninth-deck corridor and headed out to the starboard promenade. Cold wind whipped off the Atlantic, making the hairs on his arms prickle. Reese pinned his tie against his chest as they rounded the corner.

The walkie-talkie on Hendricks's belt chirped. She brought it up against her cheek and pressed the Transmit button. "Go for Hendricks."

"Tracy, we just got a hit on that passenger you were looking for," Thomas St. Clair's voice crackled through the speaker. "Colin Fisher? His key card was swiped at the Surfside Café two minutes ago."

"Copy that. Stand by, Tom. We may need you depending on how this goes down."

"Ten-four. Standing by."

Hendricks clipped the walkie back to her belt and turned to Reese. "Let's get up there before we lose him."

"You took the words right out of my mouth."

The Surfside Café was located on the fourteenth deck of the forward ship, second from the top. Situated above the navigational bridge, it offered some of the finest views on board the *Atlantia*. Twenty-four bistro-style tables sat perched against a huge glass window, with more tables outside on the open-air portion of the deck.

Reese and Hendricks headed past the kitchen entrance. The early lunch rush had already kicked in as line cooks busily prepared turkey clubs and chocolate croissants.

Families sat together around the barstools, sipping smoothies and stirring coffee.

Hendricks nudged Reese and pointed beyond the glass window. Outside, at the table nearest the bow of the ship, Colin Fisher sat alone, clutching an espresso, gazing at the Atlantic.

They headed outside to speak to the guest. It became clear why none of the other diners had chosen an outdoor table. The strong gusts of wind on the ninth-floor promenade were nearly doubled up here.

"Mr. Fisher?" Reese yelled over the wind. "Colin Fisher?"

"Yes? Who are you?" he asked.

Fisher turned, took one look at the two of them, then peered back toward the open sea. Clearly, he wasn't the type to be intimidated by a uniform.

"My name is Jake Reese; I'm head of security for the *Atlantia*. And this is Officer Tracy Hendricks."

Fisher groaned. "If this is about what happened in the casino, I don't want to get into it. I've let it go."

"What happened in the casino?" Hendricks questioned.

"Nothing. Forget I said anything."

The officers tentatively approached his table. Fisher sipped the espresso with his left hand. His right hand was tucked into a jacket pocket.

Reese held his hand an inch from his holster as he closed in. "Mr. Fisher," he said, "do you mind if we ask you a few questions?"

"Questions? Why? I didn't do anything."

The two officers finally stepped in front of him. Fisher had small pockmarks across his face and a crooked nose. He glared at them through his two ash-gray eyes.

Doesn't look like Butler, Reese thought.

Hendricks always had a knack for facial recognition. Reese glanced across to her. She studied the man's face, then signaled with the tiniest shake of her head.

She's not sure.

"You're not in any trouble, Mr. Fisher," Reese said. "We just wanted to see how your vacation is going, since you're not here with any friends or family. You're traveling alone, isn't that right?"

"So are you," Fisher fired back.

"That's a good point."

Fisher sighed and took another sip of his drink. "I come on these trips for my wife. She passed a few years back. She loved being out here on the water. We used to celebrate our anniversary on the *Atlantia*. I promised her when she was dying that I would not stop, you know, living."

Reese made a mental note to search the public records for Mrs. Fisher's obituary.

Fisher's eyes teared up, and he continued, "So, I still come every year. Keeping up the tradition we had, in honor of her."

"You have our sincere condolences on her passing," Hendricks said earnestly. "We're sorry to ask, but do you happen to have any identification on you? A driver's license we could take a look at?"

"Here we go again. Did you two send that woman earlier today? She working with you?"

"Woman? What woman?" Reese asked.

"That crazy lady in the casino. She was asking me all the same questions you're asking me now."

Reese knew exactly who had confronted Fisher.

Maria Fontana.

Even without access to security intel and a team of eyes on the ground, Fontana was seemingly one step ahead of him in this investigation.

"She's not with us," Reese said. "We hope no one from the security team has caused you any problems."

"You mean besides you two? Right now? I heard about all the trouble you've been having with that room on the eighth floor. I heard you all found a buncha dead cats in there. If you think I had anything to do with that, you're crazy. I love cats."

Reese tried not to laugh. How he wished that's what they'd found.

Rumors really do fly.

"Mr. Fisher, quick question," Hendricks said. "What do you do for a living?"

"I'm an exterminator in Jersey."

"Is that right? Well, that's a strong midwestern accent if I've ever heard one."

Fisher rolled his eyes. "Minnesota. Born and bred. I moved out to Jersey back in 1999 when I met my wife. Stayed there ever since."

"Got it," Reese said. "What kind of pests do you regularly exterminate out there in New Jersey? Anything interesting?"

"Oh, well, let's see now . . . grain beetles, weevils, hornets, silverfish, brown-banded cockroaches, springtails, dog ticks, fleas, clover mites—you name it, I'll kill it. Wait, is that what this is about? Is there an infestation on board? Jesus, you got bedbugs, don't you?"

"No, no. Nothing like that. I'm sorry we wasted your time, sir. Please enjoy the rest of your trip."

Fisher took his balled fist out of his pocket. Unclenched it, revealing a wedding ring. He gave the silver band a soft kiss and stood from his chair as well. "Well, if there's nothing I can do for you, I'll be on my way now."

Reese and Hendricks stepped back as Fisher moved toward the café.

"Like I said, I'm here for my wife," he muttered as he passed. "To remember her. Not to be harassed by other people. And if it's all right with you, I'd prefer to be left alone."

25

Messina's, the Italian restaurant on the eleventh deck, played soothing Sicilian music over dim lighting. Maria and her family were seated at a quiet table near the back. Since the restaurant was not on the all-inclusive plan, only half the tables were filled.

Good choice. Fewer people in here. Fewer eyes.

Even though the meal was sure to be expensive, being surrounded by thousands of other passengers in the main dining hall sounded like Maria's own personal hell.

The twins squirmed in their seats and pushed away the two coloring book sets. The waiter had tried his best, but they were much too old for that nonsense.

Maria swirled the straw around in her ice water, keeping

her eyes down. She felt a pang of guilt for leaving her family earlier in the day to search for Butler. But it felt nice to be back with them now. The family time she'd always treasured.

Everyone together.

Everyone safe.

A waiter walked by, carrying a plate of steamy mushroom risotto. The smell of truffle oil and shallots filled Maria's nostrils. Her stomach growled. Unsurprising because she loved the dish and couldn't remember her last meal.

"Ah, jeez, I can't decide!" Steve said, dipping another chunk of bread into the olive oil and balsamic mixture on the table. "Everything on the menu sounds so good."

The same waiter circled back around to them and took their orders. The twins both wanted spaghetti and meatballs, but Steve insisted they try something new. Maria ordered the risotto and a margherita pizza for the table, already predicting the kids wouldn't like the shrimp dish Steve ordered on their behalf. The waiter jotted each order down on his pad and flitted away to the kitchen.

"So . . . how was everyone's day?" Maria asked.

Chloe and Christopher remained quiet, twiddling with the napkins in their laps, probably wishing they had their Nintendo Switches with them.

"I had a good time," Steve said, trying to stay upbeat. "Cleaned up the cabin. Got to catch up on some reading out on the balcon—"

"Today was the worst!" Christopher spat. "We were stuck inside all day. I wanted to go rock climbing."

"Yeah," Chloe added, "if you're gonna take off on your own, Mom, at least let us hang out by the pool."

"Listen, I'm sorry I was gone," Maria said soothingly. "And I'm sorry you were stuck inside, but it was important that we keep you safe. Besides, it was way too windy to go rock climbing. Tomorrow will be different. We'll all go wherever you guys want, I promise."

The twins pouted. Not even a slice of pizza would patch things up at this point.

"And whoever came by today was *loud*," Chloe said.

What?

"Came by today?"

"Yeah."

Maria bolted in her seat. She stared at her fiancé intensely. "What do you mean? Who came by today, Steve?"

"Oh, um, it was that guy. Uh, Reese. That's his name. He and another security person," Steve sputtered. "Came by for a few minutes and asked a few questions; it was no big deal."

"The head of security was in *our* cabin? Why? What did he say? What did he ask? And what did *you* say?"

"I mean, just normal stuff."

"*Normal* stuff?" Maria pressed. "Tell me exactly what they said, Steve."

"I don't know. They asked about us. Our relationship. How long we'd been together. Just regular questions. Nothing too crazy."

Reese is investigating us? *Investigating* me?

"Why on earth were they asking you any questions to begin with?" Maria demanded. "And more importantly, why on earth did you answer them?"

"Why *wouldn't* I answer them, Maria?" Steve shot back. "We have nothing to hide, right? What would you have me do, just slam the door in their faces? Something tells me they don't need a warrant on a cruise ship. I was just trying to help."

Maria shook her head in disbelief at what she was hearing.

That damn Reese. Wasting time.

He should be focused on Butler.

Not Steve and me, for Christ's sake.

"Look, I didn't know what they wanted," Steve said. "I thought maybe something had happened to *you*! Lord knows where you'd been all day."

Steve lowered his voice as the hostess passed close by, heading for a nearby table.

A middle-aged man pushing an elderly lady in a wheelchair followed closely behind. The woman had a tube going into her nose, feeding oxygen from the tank attached to her chair.

Steve stood up and maneuvered a few chairs out of the way for the woman and man to get through. The restaurant clearly had too many tables squeezed together. The hostess headed to the corner of the restaurant and got them settled. Steve stayed to help shift the chairs back into position.

Even in the middle of getting chewed out, Steve still wants to be helpful.

Maybe I'm overreacting.

Maria took a deep breath. This was just Steve's nature. Regardless of the circumstances, he always wanted to feel useful. He probably got a kick out of being questioned by the security officers. Felt like he was a part of the investigation.

As Steve helped assist the other table, Maria turned back to the kids and continued the conversation. "So after I left you guys, what did you do?"

"I dunno," Chloe replied. "We played checkers and then watched some TV. I guess we played Jenga too. By the time Steve left, we were so bored that we just took a nap. I didn't even get much sleep."

The blood drained from Maria's face.

By the time Steve what?

"Wait, hold on a second." Maria leaned in toward her daughter. "Steve left? As in, left the cabin? He left you two alone in there?"

Chloe and Christopher shared a glance. They looked like they were debating whether they had just said something wrong.

"It wasn't too long. Chloe and I stayed inside just like he said. We were good, I promise."

Maria's focus shifted to Steve. The affection she'd felt just moments ago had transformed into blind fury.

Steve smiled down at the table with the elderly woman and presumably her son. The man nodded back and thanked him.

He left my kids alone? After I explicitly told him not to?

Steve shimmied his way back to their table and plopped back down in his seat.

"So. Anyone else already thinking about dessert?" he asked cheerfully. "I say we get ice cream sundaes."

Maria stared back at him. Silent. Heartbroken.

The one person on this ship I trusted . . .

And he lied to me.

26

ONE HOUR LATER . . .

The man inspected his knuckles. Rubbed red and raw. The night wind that swept across the ocean threatened to knock him off with each gale. He clung to the cold metal bars of the balcony and hoisted himself up to the next floor, kicking his legs with ease up onto the ledge above.

Over a hundred feet below him, waves crashed against the lower hull of the *Atlantia*. Even at this height, specks of sea salt licked at the man's heels.

He'd planned the timing perfectly. Most of the ship was off enjoying dinner or the wide array of scheduled shows and events of the evening. A string of empty cabins and the occasional sleeping passengers had given him a clear path on his way up.

Every balcony he climbed past had the drapes drawn or the lights off. The man went completely unnoticed in the darkness, straddling the starboard side of the vast ship. He had trained for this specific activity for quite some time. Enjoyed the precision of his movements, expertly taming the unpredictability of the waves rocking the vessel.

He pulled himself up onto another deck. Smooth glass dividers on either side of the balconies signaled the limits of each stateroom. Their design made them difficult to traverse.

But he didn't need to cross over to any of the adjacent cabins left or right.

He'd picked this column of cabins carefully.

And he knew exactly where he was going.

The muscles in his arms ached, but he propelled himself forward. Glanced down at the bloodthirsty and frigid swell of ocean.

He felt nothing. No fear. No adrenaline.

Just calm.

Just the task at hand.

Desire to finish what he'd started.

He towed himself up onto the next deck.

Muffled voices bled out from the cabin above.

He peeked over the lowest rung of the railing.

Nobody on the balcony. The caged light above switched off. The drapes pulled shut. Only dark shadows of the people inside, seemingly in a heated debate.

Perfection.

He pulled himself up to the balcony and swung his leg over the railing. His feet slapped against the ground. He slunk against the wall, dousing himself in darkness. Undetected. Anonymous.

Inside the cabin, a man and a woman argued aggressively. The dynamics of their voices fluctuated up and down. He tuned his ears to pick their cadence out above the rush of the wind and the sound of the water.

"I can't believe you!" the woman shouted.

It was quiet for a moment.

The man flattened his back against the balcony divider and positioned himself in just a way where he could see between the slits of the curtain.

Inside the cabin, the woman had taken up a position of dominance. He sat on the edge of the bed. She stood over the man she was arguing with. Another snippet of sound snuck through the thick glass door.

"Tell me why! What was so important?"

He crouched down low. Silently, he scanned his surroundings on the balcony. Something caught his eye.

A set of bathing suits sat in a heap on one of the lounge chairs.

Careless.

One pair of men's trunks. A woman's one-piece. And then . . . something else.

An unexpected gift.

Two children's swimsuits.

Both of them stiff and washed out from sitting in the sun all day.

Bone dry.

A tingle of electricity ran through his entire body.

He leaned in close and inhaled. The scent of chlorine clung to the polyester. He grabbed the girl's set first, balling it up into a tight, spherical wad of strings and cloth. Then he took the boy's trunks, folding them up neatly and stowing them in his waistband.

He smiled as the voices inside the cabin quieted down.

In the far distance, a single bolt of lightning split the sky. A few seconds later, a quiet roll of thunder boomed across the ocean.

Without hesitation, he positioned himself on the safety railing, being sure to get his footing. He reached up to the next balcony above and heaved.

Hoisting himself upward.

And completely out of sight.

27

Maria stood in line at the coffee shop, patiently waiting. The wind from yesterday had finally died down, and more people were out and about on the pool deck. Bright sunshine cast the entire ship in a flaxen glow. Behind the counter ahead of her, baristas yanked levers in unison on the high-pressure pumps, sending steaming blasts of espresso into each mug.

Physically, Maria felt calmer than yesterday. Clearer. More at ease. Her heart rate had mostly returned to normal, and the sweating in her palms had subsided. Going nearly two days without any sleep had certainly taken its toll.

She'd managed to get a few hours of shut-eye on the couch, sneaking out of bed after Steve had dozed off. Sleeping next to him just didn't feel right after the argument they'd had.

She still couldn't believe he'd left the kids alone, even if his intentions were good. He'd explained that he left the cabin, looking for her out of concern. That he was gone for less than an hour, not daring to keep up his search any longer because of the kids.

No matter what, he still should not have left.

She wondered how much of what she felt yesterday had been paranoia.

Perhaps Steve was right . . .

Regardless, Maria had made good on her promise to the twins, not wanting to ruin another day for them. First thing that morning, when they all woke up, she and Steve took the kids to the zip line that spanned across the aft part of deck fourteen.

They'd been the first in line for the day, right when the ride opened. The sound of Chloe and Christopher laughing with glee as they each took the plunge made Maria forget the anxiety, even if only for a few minutes.

We can still make this good. Still create some new memories.

She tapped her foot, not out of impatience for the coffee but out of unconscious instinct. Maybe a bit of residual nervousness from the previous events.

The twins were across the deck with Steve, right by the giant chess set—within Maria's view, of course. They watched the game currently in progress, their eyes lighting up each time one of the life-size pieces slammed into another.

Everyone in the coffee line shuffled forward a couple of steps.

Maria glanced to her left.

The wheelchair-bound lady from last night had been parked on the outskirts of the queue.

The woman recognized her too. She met Maria's gaze and shook her head. "They're piddlin' around up there! I'll be a bag of dust before they get this darned coffee out!"

"Oh, my apologies. Are you in line?"

"No, no. That's all right, darlin'. You're too sweet." The woman extended a frail, wrinkled hand with a smile. "Catherine Davies. Nice to meet you."

Maria gave it a gentle shake. Catherine had a thick Southern accent. It dripped with the buttery, honey-golden sense of hospitality that a native New Yorker like Maria couldn't dare try to imitate.

Her icy-white hair was cropped short to her head, but her bright, dentured smile gleamed with the energy of someone half her age. Despite the breathing tubes in her nose and oxygen tank strapped to her wheelchair, a certain joie de vivre surrounded Catherine.

"Who's getting your coffee?" Maria said.

"I've got somebody up there gettin' it for me." The woman pointed toward a man near the front of the line. The same one from yesterday who had pushed her to the dining table.

"Is that your son?" Maria asked.

"Oh no, that's my nurse, Todd. Sweet man."

Todd was tall and lean. He'd just reached the counter and exchanged his key card for two mugs of whipped cream–topped lattes.

Within seconds, he'd shimmied his way through the crowded lines to where Catherine and Maria stood. He smiled widely at Maria and carefully placed the steaming mug into Catherine's shaky hands.

"Careful now, that's real hot, darlin'," he said with the same swampy drawl as Catherine's. He looked at Maria. "Well, hello there! Oh, dang, I'm so sorry. I shoulda brought back three."

Maria politely waved him off. "No, that's all right. Really—"

"Lemme go see if they can make up an extra one for me real quick." He flashed Maria another warm smile and darted back to the counter.

Maria turned back to Catherine. "You weren't kidding. He's a sweetheart."

"Oh, he's the best caretaker I've ever had! By a long shot. Been real good to me too. They raise them right in Georgia."

Maria smiled at the woman. "I'm trying to raise them right in New York too. I'm here with my two kids, right over there, and my fiancé."

"Isn't that lovely?" Catherine replied. "We all deserve a nice vacation from time to time. That's why I brought Todd along with me; he deserved it. Especially after the year he's been through. My goodness, bless his soul."

Catherine laid her free hand against her chest. "He's been in and out of the hospital more than me!"

"I'm so sorry to hear that. Is he sick?"

"He don't talk about it much. But golly, he's had more surgeries than I've had husbands."

Maria burst out laughing at the comment. Catherine sure had a way with words. She glanced over at Todd, who looked back and smiled, holding up another coffee. He had successfully sweet-talked his way into a third latte, free of charge.

Suddenly, a distant shriek rang out through the café.

At first, Maria thought it was a child. The joyous shrills of young kids was something she was used to. Even more so since being on this cruise ship.

But this scream was different.

And it didn't stop. More cries followed the first.

Loud.

Deep.

Much deeper than a child's voice.

It sounded like a full-grown man screaming.

Maria whipped around. Steve and the twins stood by the chess set. Still there. Still safe.

The shrieks rang out from the opposite direction. Somewhere alongside the other end of the lido deck. By the hot tubs. Everyone in the café strained their necks to see what was causing the commotion.

When the screams didn't stop, the fear began spreading. All around Maria, people began to panic. Families scurried out of the coffee shop and away from the chaotic sound. Chairs were bumped into and knocked over as a stampede formed in the blink of an eye.

Todd dropped his mug at the counter, shattering it on the floor. He ran back to the friendly old woman, gripped the handles of her wheelchair, and followed suit, pushing his patient away from the dangerous situation that was quickly taking over.

Not knowing what was happening, everyone in the café bolted in the other direction. Away from the source of the commotion.

But with no time to spare, and without hesitation, Maria turned and ran *toward* the screams.

28

Reese practically flew down the staircase. His walkie-talkie chirped over and over again on his hip, calls frantically pouring in. But there was no need to answer. The mass of fleeing passengers running past him signaled to Reese exactly where he needed to go.

He'd been on his way to the bridge to debrief with Captain DeForest when he'd heard the first ominous scream. The rumble of footsteps and mass hysteria that followed had snapped him into action.

Reese pulled his pistol from his holster and gripped it low, down by his hip, pointing the barrel toward the floor as he ran.

He pushed and shoved his way through the charging herd

of terrified passengers. A few panicked eyes in the crowd recognized his uniform and pointed behind them as they ran, signaling in the direction of the danger. Reese shouldered his way through the pack until he finally reached the lido deck.

The entire floor was utter chaos.

Screeching mothers desperately tried to pull their children out of the main pool. A man ran past the rinse-off station, slipped on the wet deck, and plummeted face-first into the wall.

Thomas St. Clair rushed to his front. "This way, sir!"

The look on his face said a thousand words. And none were good.

St. Clair stormed over to the serving area by the hot tubs. Other guards stationed near the aft deck tried to move the crowd away.

Reese and St. Clair rounded the corner and came upon the huddled circle of stunned passengers. They all stood rooted to the spot, planted in the ground by an unseen force. Some sobbed uncontrollably. Others screamed in short bursts.

"Everyone move back!" Reese shouted, not knowing what he was walking into. "Move back. *Right now!*"

He elbowed his way through and finally broke into the clearing. In front of him was an industrial-size soft-serve ice cream machine. A cruise ship employee, perched on top of a stepladder, overlooked the open vat on top of the machine.

A mechanic by the look of his uniform.

Reese switched his focus to the deck.

In the center of the clearing, a cylindrical shape, slathered in ice cream, sat on the boards.

What is that?

He approached cautiously, squinting to get a better look.

No.

It can't be.

But it was.

A severed arm.

Small. With a thin wrist and delicate fingers. Laid bare in the middle of the pool deck. For everyone to see.

The melted vanilla ice cream that coated the limb was a pearly, milky white. No hint of red in the mixture.

Not a single drop of blood.

Reese fixed his attention back on the wide-eyed mechanic.

"What the hell happened?" Reese asked. "What happened?"

The worker stood there. Frozen. Mouth agape. Clearly in a state of shock.

Reese grabbed him by the collar of his jumpsuit and yanked him down onto the floor.

"I-I-I-I don't know!" the mechanic finally sputtered. "I, uh—there was, uh—there was something stuck—stuck in the machine. I-I-I just pulled it out. And—"

"Move out of the way," Reese commanded, pushing him toward the rest of the passengers. "Stand where I can see you! St. Clair, hold him!"

Thomas grabbed the woozy mechanic by his shoulders and propped him upright.

"Who called for the mechanic?" Reese bellowed, silencing the crowd. "Who called?"

Another crewmember sheepishly raised her hand. The passengers around her parted so Reese could get a clear view. The name tag and vest she wore suggested she was part of the dining team.

"Don't move. You both stay here."

She erupted into tears. Within seconds, St. Clair had hands on both of them.

"Now I need all of you to step back," Reese instructed. "Please. Step back!"

Everyone followed his order.

Reese lifted his foot onto the first rung of the ladder, gripping the sides for extra support. He carefully climbed up each step.

Once he reached the top, he took a deep breath of the cool midmorning air and peered down into the vat.

A swirling mess of cream, limbs, and hair rotated in the large basin.

A torso.

A shoulder.

A thigh.

The dismembered parts of a child, crammed haphazardly inside the soft-serve ice cream machine.

One of the small feet was lodged against the metal stirring rod, causing it to jam and spatter droplets of dairy substance up toward the rim.

Reese lurched back, almost falling off the ladder.

Bile filled his mouth.

He fought back the urge to vomit.

Another murder.

Another child.

He stepped down off the ladder in a daze. His vision threatened to black out. Out of the corner of his eye, the sight of two familiar faces pushing through the crowd brought him back to reality.

It was Captain DeForest with Hendricks following closely behind. Reese snapped upright and caught his breath in his throat. Regaining his composure.

"Everyone, clear the area!" Reese shouted. "Passengers, go back to your cabins and lock the doors! Crewmembers, head to your muster stations immediately!"

For a moment, nobody reacted. The frightened eyes of the crowd fell on Captain DeForest, waiting for the senior man's response.

"You heard him," Captain DeForest said. "Everyone move!"

Hendricks instantly jumped into action, directing the remaining passengers and crewmembers out of the area and into the aft stairwell.

St. Clair continued to hold on to the mechanic and dining

worker. Both appeared in a state of shock. Neither, in Reese's mind, were immediate suspects, but they had to be certain.

DeForest stepped toward him. "What the hell happened here, Reese?"

Goddamn it.

Reese hated to admit it. He hated even more that this had happened under his watch.

Maria Fontana was right.

He leaned in to the captain's ear and lowered his voice. "Captain, we need to lock down the entire ship, immediately," Reese said, praying no one else could hear his next words.

"We have a killer on board."

29

Maria and her family moved between the crowd of passengers. The entire ship had transformed into pure chaos. Confusion and fear reigned. Security guards stationed on each floor suddenly looked like air traffic controllers, waving their arms in huge circles, trying to calmly direct passengers back to their cabins. Hundreds of people packed the stairs as everyone tried to make it safely to their respective floors.

"Someone has a gun!"

"I heard it's a bomb threat!"

"No, no! It's just a safety drill!"

Rumors flew back and forth between the horde of passengers in the aft stairwell leading away from the pool deck.

But Maria knew the truth. She'd been there. She'd seen the

severed limb pulled from the ice cream dispenser. Watched as Reese arrived on the scene. The horrific realization that she knew exactly what was happening.

He's here.

Butler's here.

And he's done hiding.

Now, she and Steve hustled down the stairs, each with their arms wrapped tightly around the twins. Maria wanted to teleport back to dry land. Knowing that her children and Wyatt Butler were in the same place made her skin crawl. But adrenaline made her move. She powered to the twelfth floor and rounded the corner.

The captain's voice boomed over the speaker, *"Passengers, please return to your cabins in a calm and orderly fashion. Please, do not panic."*

"What's going on?" one woman in the herd yelled back to the PA system.

"I repeat, passengers, please return to your cabins. HMS Atlantia *crew, please report to your muster stations. Charlie, Charlie, Charlie."*

Maria had no idea what the code *Charlie, Charlie, Charlie* meant, but it was easy to imagine, considering the earlier scene. She needed to get to Officer Reese. Get to the captain, even. Tell them everything she knew.

But Chloe and Christopher.

They need to be safe.

Securing them was her first, second, and third priority. Stopping Butler could wait a few more minutes.

They need *to be safe.*

Steve had sprung into action the moment the first scream rang out by the ice cream dispenser. He'd scooped up the twins and packed them all tightly behind the cash bar before Maria could rejoin them. He'd waited for her. So they could head back as a family.

"Mommy?" her son said.

The sound of Christopher's voice ripped her back to the present. It was a name he only used for her when he thought he was in trouble. *Mommy.* A sweet, nostalgic name, from their years as toddlers.

"Yes, baby?" Maria said.

"Is . . . is the ship sinking?"

"No, sweetheart. Shhh. Shhh. You're okay. We're okay." Maria pulled his head in close to her chest and ran her fingers through his hair. Chloe quietly sobbed next to him. She clung to Steve's T-shirt with one hand and nervously bit at the nails on her other.

"Hey, guys," Steve said. "It's gonna be okay. Everything's gonna be fine."

A voice in the packed stairwell rose above the rest. "Patrick? Patrick?"

Maria spotted the shouting woman down on the landing in front of them. She yelled back up toward the stairs.

Looking for someone. She'd stopped dead in her tracks, causing a buildup of angry passengers behind her.

"Hey, keep moving, lady!"

"*Patrick?*" the woman yelled again with growing despair in her voice.

Maria's heart sank. She'd seen the arm they'd pulled from the vat. It was small. Certainly taken from a child. She prayed it didn't belong to this woman's son.

"Momma!"

Moments later, a little boy appeared at the top of the staircase. Maria turned her head, following the mother's path as she sprinted back up the stairs and scooped her son up into her arms.

Debris had cluttered the stairwell. Loose flip-flops and dropped hats. Maria's mind flashed back to the images of the courtroom. The eerie, mismatched clothing at each crime scene.

He's created the perfect environment for himself.

Children are being separated from their parents.

All this chaos. The mayhem. She had no doubt in her mind.

It will push Butler to strike again.

He won't be able to control himself.

After one more flight of stairs, what seemed like an eternity later, they reached the ninth floor. Two security guards shouted out the room numbers for each wing, hoping to minimize the number of frantic passengers running into mistaken hallways.

Steve and Maria bumped past people. The stateroom corridor had always felt small and tight. Claustrophobic, even. But now, with dozens of families struggling to get into their cabins, the entire hallway was like a floating tomb.

The two of them formed a shield around the twins, barreling through anyone who stood between them and cabin 925. They slunk by one last family.

We made it.

Maria slammed her key card into the slot and watched as the light on the handle switched from red to green. She opened the door and hurried the twins inside. Steve ducked in just as Maria shut the door behind her. In one fluid motion, she slid the dead bolt into place and yanked the chain across the threshold.

The room looked exactly as they'd left it. Everything perfectly in place. Whatever housekeeping that was scheduled to come that afternoon hadn't made their rounds yet. She glanced up to the clock hanging on the wall.

11:07 a.m.

Maria rushed over to the sliding-glass door leading out to the balcony and threw down the blinds. Steve hustled into the smaller room and drew the curtains before marching into the master bedroom to do the same.

Finally, in the safety of the cabin, the twins broke down. All the tears that had been building up finally released themselves in a torrent of cries and shaking. Chloe and Christopher curled up into two tiny balls on the couch and shivered, terrified and confused.

"Shhh, it's okay, baby. It's okay," Maria said, kneeling down in front of the kids. She put a hand on each of their backs and rubbed gently. "We're safe now. You're safe."

But something seemed off.

The door to the bathroom.

It was closed. Shut tightly.

Her grip on the kids instinctively stiffened.

Was that closed when we left?

"Steve," Maria whispered. "*Steve.* Get in here."

He came bounding out of the master bedroom. "What? What is it?"

Maria silently nodded toward the bathroom. Steve glanced over to the door, immediately recognizing her concern.

She mouthed the words to him. *Did you close that?*

He thought about it for a moment with a furrowed brow and then quietly mouthed back, *I don't remember.*

Maria moved her body between the kids on the couch and the door, shielding them from whatever, or whoever, was inside that bathroom.

Steve stepped toward the countertop and silently unplugged the cabin telephone. He lifted the heavy mount high above his head, wielding the phone like a weapon, and took slow deliberate steps back toward the bathroom.

Maria's heart hammered against her chest. She needed to stay on alert. In case Steve and his telephone weren't enough.

In one quick motion, Steve flung open the bathroom door. It swung hard on its hinges and slapped against the wall on the opposite side.

Empty. The shower stall was wide open, and the toilet seat was left up. Probably Christopher's doing.

Maria and her fiancé shared a sigh of relief. As much as she'd wanted to curl up on the couch with her kids and spend the lockdown here, she knew that wasn't an option. She had a role to play in all of this. There was only one thing she knew for certain.

This isn't over.

Not by a long shot.

He's not nearly done.

30

Neon-yellow caution tape bordered the entire lido deck. What had been a place of joy and relaxation less than an hour ago had quickly devolved into a full-blown crime scene.

Reese paced back and forth around the hot tubs. Time was his only valuable resource. Whoever murdered this child, whoever did this, had deliberately put the body here. In one of the most public places on the entire ship, on purpose.

He knew we'd find it.

He wanted *us to find it.*

Reese wrestled with this realization. In all his years of police work in Miami, he knew that a public act of criminality was often just a portion of a much larger statement. First, it was Finch's head. Left in a closed-off cabin for only the security team to find. Then, the child overboard to arouse suspicions. Now this. The killer was getting bolder.

Speed is of the essence.

And hopefully, with the ship being on lockdown, that would slow the killer's next plans, whatever they might be.

Reese had sent Hendricks to the operations room to try to assemble as many security units as possible, regardless of their assigned shifts. He instructed her to put a call into the cruise line first, followed by the U.S. and UK coast guards. After that, she was to get in contact with the FBI and MI5. Protocol for a murder on a cruise ship was murky at best, and in his decade serving on the *Atlantia,* Reese had never seen one on board. A welcome respite from those horrific days on the force in Miami.

Most cruise ship deaths were your typical causes: heart attacks, stroke, alcohol poisoning, preexisting medical conditions. But something this sinister was uncharted territory. He'd need as much help as he could get.

Even if that meant making this an international case.

With the majority of the guards busy securing passengers safely in their cabins, only a select team remained at the crime scene. Officers Thomas St. Clair and the younger Carl Lystad carefully disassembled the ice cream dispenser, unscrewing the bolts in place and meticulously pulling off layer after layer of metal plating.

Two other officers—Timmins and Shea—had the tougher

job. They'd laid out a plastic tarp on the ground nearby and delicately placed the severed arm into position. It was their task to arrange the pieces of the corpse in the order they were pulled from the machine.

Slowly but surely, the body began to take shape. The torso was laid out first. Then the pelvis. Upper arms next. The shins were matched with the feet. Then the thighs and the forearms.

It was a young girl.

Each piece of her covered in the melting leftover ice cream.

Fourteen or fifteen, by the looks of her.

Jesus Christ.

"Sir . . ."

Reese looked to his left. Thomas St. Clair stood next to him, yanking the ice cream–coated latex gloves off his hands.

"Sir, at this point, I think getting any fingerprints off the body might be an impossibility. Not only that, but passengers have been touching the ice cream machine all day, every day. What's the point?"

Reese silently nodded. He knew in his gut that fingerprints wouldn't be the make or break in catching this killer.

A hush fell over the entire deck as Officer Timmins carried the last piece of the girl out of the vat and onto the plastic tarp. Shivers shot through Reese's spine.

Her head.

Chunks of matted hair and globs of ice cream obscured most of her features. But her bright green eyes shone through as clear as day. Her eyelids had been sadistically propped open with staples. Maybe while still alive . . .

God have mercy on us.

As her full body was assembled, a sickening feeling overtook the personnel at the scene. Lystad shared his queasiness as he dry-heaved. The color had all but drained from Officer Shea's face.

Most of his staff were used to working concerts. Conventions. Comic-Cons. Off this ship, they were little more than your everyday security guards. One even worked part-time at Target. Reese knew they were not equipped for the task at hand—hunting down and stopping a murderer. But he had to hold the team together.

He knew their pain, though. Empathized. He remembered the moment when he'd seen his first body. It was early in his career. A car crash. Single-vehicle accident. The driver had mangled himself in a heap of twisted metal and blood after wrapping his sports car around a massive pine tree. Despite it being two decades ago, Reese remembered every inch of the corpse. The image had seared itself into his brain.

And then he remembered his last case as a police officer in Miami. The case that ended his career . . .

31

ELEVEN YEARS EARLIER . . .

The mercury had already risen to ninety-seven degrees, and it wasn't even noon yet in Miami.

Officer Reese and his partner, Officer Annalise Michaels, went to investigate a domestic violence report on Fifty-first Street in Model City, ironically named given how dilapidated and dangerous the neighborhood was.

The third frantic 911 call in the past few months from the same woman.

Twenty-eight-year-old Isabella Fernandez. She was a mother of two children, nine-year-old Emma and five-year-old Aiden. Her on-again, off-again boyfriend and father of her kids, Alex Martin, was a real piece of work. Alcoholic, addicted to H, and had put Isabella in the hospital twice from assault.

But Alex Martin wasn't anything new. In fact, Reese had dealt with at least a dozen other Alex Martins just in the last six months. An unfortunate reality. Sadly commonplace in a metropolis like Miami. Despicable, ignorant men who abused and exerted their power over the women who cared for them. It was something he could never understand.

He and Michaels had been nearby investigating a trespassing complaint when the call from dispatch came in. They pulled up to the house a few minutes later and stepped out of the cruiser into the blazing sun. The sounds of rara drums and jangling guitars from the nearby blocks of neighboring Little Haiti echoed down the street. Despite the heat, it was a gorgeous day in Miami. Another day in supposed paradise. The turquoise sky hung above the city like another ocean.

Reese and Michaels climbed the rickety wooden steps up to the front door. Mold had overtaken every corner of the home's frame. The property seemed like it hadn't been repaired since the last hurricane that'd blown through two years earlier. Michaels rested her palm on the butt of her gun clipped in to her tactical belt.

The two officers reached the front door and stopped. They listened for a moment, all but pressing their ears against the peeling paint on the door.

Quiet.

Reese banged his outermost knuckle against the door three times. "Hello? MPD. Is anyone home?"

Another moment passed.

Silence.

"Hello? Ms. Fernandez?"

Reese reached for the doorknob and gave it a twist. It wouldn't turn.

Locked.

"Police. Open up."

Silence.

He and Michaels exchanged a glance.

Not a good sign.

Simultaneously, the two officers drew their pistols. Just as Reese reached for the knob again, a sound from within the house stopped him short.

A thump.

Then another thump.

Then screams.

Reese rammed his shoulder against the flimsy door.

It battered open.

Squeals came from the corner of the living room. The kids. Little Emma and Aiden. They shrieked at the top of their lungs, tears cascading down their cheeks. Both cowering between the corner of the couch and a broken floor lamp, trying to make themselves even smaller than they already were.

A violent struggle had broken out on the floor. A man and a woman wrestled in a vicious brawl, swinging fists, scratching, gouging, and kicking as they reached for something buried beneath them.

"Don't move!" Officer Michaels shouted out. *"Don't move! Hands up where I can see them!"*

Her voice distracted the man just long enough for the struggling woman to land a slugging punch to his jaw, sending him a few inches backward.

It gave her space to grab what she'd been looking for.

Slowly, Isabella rose up from the floor, giving Reese his first good look at her.

Bruises covered her body. Worse than any other domestic violence dispute he'd been called to investigate. The skin around her right eye had swollen and puffed up. Red blotches of blood and lesions dotted around her collarbone. Raised lumps speckled every other inch of her exposed arms. Fresh blood trickled from a slit above her eye and from a busted lower lip. Who knows what bones were broken inside her.

She had a manic look in her eyes.

The final straw had snapped in her mind.

And now she stood tall. Pointing the Glock 41 at Alex. Though her legs jittered and trembled, the gun in her hand stayed perfectly steady. Her sights locked on the sorry excuse for a man crouched on the floor across from her.

"*Help!* This *fucking bitch* is trying to *kill me*!" Alex shouted in Reese's direction.

"No more . . . no more . . . no more . . . ," Isabella whispered to herself, aiming the gun squarely at the man. She never took her eyes off her target. She stared at him like a huntress. As if he were a wild animal.

Reese shifted his arms and pointed his gun in Isabella's direction. In case she decided to swing around onto him or Michaels.

"Drop the weapon! *Now!*" Reese commanded.

From the corner of the room, the children's shrieks had morphed into choking sobs.

But Isabella didn't budge. She stared ahead. Focused. Intent.

Reese didn't blame her. He'd seen this cycle of abuse too many times . . .

But nevertheless, he was a cop. He looked into the tiny sliver of her eye he could see. Empty. She was blinded by rage.

"Isabella." Reese shifted his tone to a calm temperament. "Isabella. Put the gun down. Nobody needs to get shot today."

No response.

"Listen to me, Isabella," he continued softly. "He's going to prison, I promise you. Let him rot in jail. There's no reason you have to join him."

She didn't move.

"Don't do it, Isabella," Reese said, extending out his arm to the woman.

He understood if she pulled the trigger, but hoped she wouldn't . . .

Isabella's arms finally gave out. They dropped into her lap as the gun clattered to the floor. She collapsed onto the rug in an exhausted heap.

Within half a second, Michaels jumped on the gun while Reese jumped on Alex Martin. Pinned him hard to the floor. They cuffed him, carried him down the broken stairs, and tossed him into the back of their cruiser as he screamed obscenities.

More squad cars and an ambulance converged on the scene to assist.

When Reese finally left the house, he looked up in the rearview mirror before turning off Fifty-first Street. Isabella stood on the porch. Her glare just as empty as before. She shuffled her kids back inside the decaying home.

Then . . .

Two months later, Alex Martin got out of prison on parole, went straight back to Isabella's house, and murdered her entire family.

Reese was one of the first officers on the scene that night. The entire street had been blocked off. It was a little past midnight when the call came in. He'd driven as fast as he could. Police sirens blared through the air as red and blue lights filled the sky around the home.

He peered down at the blood-soaked rug in the living room. Isabella had been shot four times. Twice in the stomach, once in the back as she tried to flee, and the final shot to the head. She had her arms wrapped around her dead kids. Both had single gunshot wounds to the head. Another unit had picked up Alex Martin a few blocks away as he fled the scene.

Of course, the piece of shit had denied everything.

Reese stared at the lifeless children.

Stared into Isabella's dead eyes.

He quit the Miami police force the next day.

32

Reese's mind drifted back to the present, trying to shake that horrific moment from so many years ago, trying to shake off the overwhelming guilt he felt.

He needed to stay focused on the new horror in front of him. "Listen up," he shouted, "someone on this boat is missing their daughter! Let's find out who. I'll be the one to tell them what has happened, no one else. Understood?"

Several of the security officers nodded.

Reese had had regular reports from the office. In the last twenty minutes, as the lockdown had been executed, dozens of calls poured in for missing children. Thankfully, most had been resolved as quickly as they came in. Frantic parents not realizing their kids were already in their cabin or brief separations during the stampede. But somewhere on this ship, Reese knew that there was a family who would never be reunited with their child.

He scanned his team.

There just aren't enough of us.

His eyes fell to the side of the deck, next to the coffee bar, where the mechanic and the dining worker who'd discovered the body were still being held. They looked shaken. Overwhelmed. But they had to give answers. He marched over to the mechanic.

"Can you tell me who had access to this machine?"

"I'm sorry?"

"Who else besides you had the key to open up the ice cream machine?"

"Key? It just . . . it just lifts off."

"Lifts off?" Reese repeated. "You're telling me anyone could have gotten into it?"

The mechanic meekly nodded.

Reese wanted to slam his fists into the wall, but maintained his composure. This investigation demanded it. He combed the corners for security cameras. From a distance, only one faced the dessert station, possibly too far away to reveal anything. But it was worth a shot. He would need to get that footage as soon as possible.

"I want a full record of every staff member who's been in

contact with this machine, whether to clean it, refill it, repair it. Everyone."

Representatives from the medical team had finally arrived on the scene, examining the machine and the body of the little girl, still coated in thick, melting layers of ice cream.

Reese approached the leader of the team, Dr. Zachary Kleiman, an older man with salt-and-pepper hair. "What can you tell me, Doc?"

"Well, the body's been completely exsanguinated. No trace of blood in the machine either," Kleiman said plainly.

Shit. Just like Finch.

"Can you tell if the exsanguination was done pre- or post-mortem?" Reese asked.

"Honestly, I won't have a good idea of that until I get her on the table," Kleiman replied. "It will take me a few hours to get her cleaned off to get a good look at everything."

A large volume of blood was clearly missing from this crime scene. If it hadn't been dumped overboard yet, finding it might be Reese's best chance.

Maybe we can find where she was bled out. A splatter of blood. A drop. Anything.

"Another thing," Kleiman added. "To separate the limbs in this fashion requires three things: experience, precision, and tools. Whoever did this has done this before."

"What about time of death?"

"That might be tricky, Jake. If she was placed into the

machine shortly after death, the refrigeration may have preserved her to some extent. Rigor mortis has clearly set in on some of the limbs, but that only takes four hours. And the cold would speed that up." Kleiman rose up from his crouched position. "This could've happened this morning. Could've been last night. Could've been a week ago if she's been on ice since then."

"Gimme something. Please, Zack."

"Like I said, I won't be able to say anything definitive until I get her downstairs."

Hendricks tapped him on the shoulder.

He spun to face her. "Tell me you got ahold of someone."

"We're too far from both the U.S. and UK coast guards to reach us by helicopter. We're on our own, Jake."

Shit.

"What about the FBI? MI5? Anything?"

"Both said there's nothing they can do until we get to shore. They both want custody of the bodies, and both want everyone in lockdown until they can do a full sweep of the ship."

That could be too late. What if this monster strikes again?

"What do you think we should do?" Hendricks asked.

He was out of options. It was clear. They needed more hands for this investigation, more experience. They needed to hunt this person down before more passengers wound up dead.

"Can we turn back?" Reese wondered aloud.

"Turn back and go where exactly?" Captain DeForest said from behind him. "We're in the middle of the goddamned Atlantic Ocean, Reese. This murderer timed this precisely. We're almost exactly halfway from shore in either direction. Six more days no matter which way we turn."

Reese felt completely overwhelmed by the situation.

"So, Mr. Reese," the captain continued pointedly, "what do you suggest we do now?"

"Sir, to be perfectly honest, this investigation requires more manpower and resources than what we've got on board."

"Well, you're all we've got. So do whatever it takes to find this maniac and stop him, Officer Reese."

He nodded at the captain. "Yes, sir. Yes, we will."

"Reese!" Officer Lystad called out from the stepladder, still positioned over the vat. "There's something else in here."

He rushed over to what was left of the dismantled ice cream machine. Lystad made room on the ladder as Reese climbed his way up. He peered down into the bottom of the vat.

A ball of cloth sat underneath the dispensing tray, mashed up and covered in ice cream.

Reese motioned to a member of the medical team. "Pass me the forceps."

He reached the metal tweezers down into the vat and lifted out one of the pieces of clothing.

A pair of boy's swim trunks.

Reese handed them to Officer Shea, who laid it out on the

tarp. He reached in again, this time pulling up the other piece of clothing.

A little girl's two-piece set, tied up together in a tight knot. From the look of it, way too small to belong to the victim.

These swimsuits belonged to smaller kids. Younger children.

Reese steadied himself on the ladder. His mind flashed back to his conversation with Maria one day earlier.

This is no coincidence.

This is the killer calling out the next victims.

"Hendricks!" Reese called out, hopping off the ladder in a hurry. "Hendricks!"

She met him in an instant. "Yes, sir?"

Reese's hands clenched into fists by his side. They couldn't turn the boat around. Nobody was coming to help. They were stuck. Stuck on board with a murderer.

And there was only one person on this ship who might have more answers.

"I need someone to go to cabin 925. ASAP."

Hendricks looked at him through a furrowed brow, but Reese held firm.

"Get me Maria Fontana."

33

In the operations room, Maria reluctantly took the seat across from Jake Reese. Hendricks had shut the door, giving the two of them some privacy. She shivered at the coolness of the air-conditioning. Glanced around at the bank of screens, stack of papers, and communication equipment. This was the first time she'd surveyed the place in detail, and it somehow gave off the impression of disorganization.

"You believe me now?" she finally asked.

He nodded. "I'm sorry I didn't listen to you sooner."

"What would you like, Mr. Reese? I'd really like to get back to my children."

"I won't keep you long, I promise." Reese opened a folder on his desk and examined the contents.

Maria fidgeted with her engagement ring. The smooth feel of the metal helped to calm her down. It brought back memories of that short period of time after the trial when she was happy. Before everything fell apart. Memories of Chloe, Christopher, and Steve.

I need to get back to them.

Even though the kids were safely locked in the stateroom with her fiancé, being away from them in this moment felt wrong. Before Officer Hendricks escorted her out of the cabin, she'd managed to play her bargaining chip: she'd refused to meet with Reese unless a security guard stayed posted outside of her cabin door.

Hendricks had huffed and then radioed in for backup. Within seconds, another officer came to cabin 925 and promised to stand guard while Maria went to see Reese.

This put her mind somewhat at ease.

"Ms. Fontana," Reese said, "as you pointed out, I'm afraid that recent events on the ship have led me to believe you might be right. We've had a crime occur on board that perfectly matches Butler's MO."

"I saw. I was on the pool deck when they pulled that poor girl out of the ice cream machine."

"Well, you didn't see everything."

Maria's heart rate spiked, afraid of what he might say next.

"At the bottom of the machine," he explained, "we found

more clothing. Children's clothing. That didn't match our victim."

Calling out his next target.

Maria swallowed hard at the revelation. "Then he's already poised to strike again."

"He's taunting us."

"Officer Reese, I warned you something like this might happen."

"I understand your frustration." He sighed, long and deep. "Believe me, I'm just as upset as you are. But I need your help figuring out the next move. If this really is Butler, or a damn good copycat, what is he going to do next? Why is he doing this? How do we stop him?"

"Well, do you have any suspects? Have you taken anyone in for questioning?"

Reese looked down at his desk, quiet, as if contemplating the crushing weight of events.

"What about that man I told you about?" she asked. "That bearded man traveling alone? Did you talk to him?"

"We did. And while I won't mention the specifics of our conversation, suffice it to say I believe him."

"Are you sure? Did you search his cabin? Check his passport? What if he lied to you? What if he—"

"His wife died," Reese said, cutting her off. "He comes on this cruise every single year as a reminder, same week. I looked him up in our system. It checks out. Ms. Fontana, you need to begin trusting me. We want the same thing."

Throughout the conversation, Reese had appeared warm and sincere. As open as he could be, considering the circumstances. This was a long way from his coldness during their first encounter.

She gave him a thin smile. "So, what leads do you have?"

"Ms. Fontana, I need your absolute word that anything we speak about is only between you and me, in order to protect the people on this ship. I am hesitant to—"

"Mr. Reese, you need to begin to trust *me.* We want the same thing."

Reese nodded after recognizing his own advice repeated back to him. He continued, "Last night, around three in the morning, one security camera on the pool deck caught this."

He swiveled a monitor in Maria's direction. Scrubbed through the footage and hit Play.

A digital timer ran in the top right of the screen. In the dark, grainy video from the pool deck's security camera, a tall figure emerged from behind the hot tubs, visibly straining to carry a large bag. The near-pitch-black night had done enough to conceal his face. He heaved the bag off his shoulder and set it down by the ice cream dispenser. Then he positioned a stepladder by the side of the machine and climbed it. Lifted the top off the vat and dumped the bag's contents into the basin.

Maria cringed, viscerally sick at the sight of pale little limbs being dumped out of the bag like old pieces of trash. Back on-screen, the moment the bag emptied, the man replaced the machine's lid, climbed down from the stepladder, and backed away. Out of camera shot in a matter of seconds.

Reese stopped the film.

"Okay," Maria said. "How about the other cameras? When he left the frame of this one?"

"That's the thing. He isn't in any other camera angle. Every entrance to the pool deck is covered. He's not in any one of them. He appears out of nowhere."

"What do you mean?"

"Look." Reese clicked through the feeds of the surrounding security cameras at the time the man was on the deck. Every single frame was empty. "He comes in from behind the hot tubs here. But we can't trace him before that moment. Nothing in the elevator bay. Nothing in the stairwells. It's like he and that bag appeared out of thin air."

"He knows where the cameras are."

"Precisely."

"He's been planning this murder," Maria said. "He knew exactly where he'd get captured on film, and he knew how to get around it. Is there some kind of passageway? Somewhere maybe out of view from the cameras that he could be using?"

"There's the Highway . . ."

"What's that?" she asked.

"It's the crew corridors that run deep in the bowels of the ship. On Deck Zero. It's how staff moves around the ship every day beneath your feet while you're all up in the sunshine. But the entire thing is covered with cameras. We checked that footage too. Nothing."

"If he has access to the Highway, does that mean . . ."

"He could be a crewmember," Reese admitted, finishing her sentence. "I'm looking into all our new hires in the past two years since the trial. But to be perfectly honest, cruise ship staff turns over very quickly. Nearly half the crew on this boat, more than eight hundred people, were not on it two years ago."

He stared at her intently, waiting for a response.

Maria took a moment to ponder the bizarreness of the situation. "Well, I don't know how he's been getting around the ship, but this vanishing act fits exactly with the evidence they presented us in the courtroom. He's somehow found a way to go completely undetected. A master of disguise, if you will. Even the eyewitnesses who saw him checking into each hotel couldn't agree on what Wyatt Butler looked like. Not a single person identified him as the killer."

"How's that possible?" Reese asked. "Different people, maybe? Could he have had multiple accomplices? Maybe we're not looking for Butler. Maybe we're looking for an apprentice. Or a disciple."

"I suppose that is a possibility."

"But . . . you don't think so?"

"No. I think he acts alone."

Reese slowly nodded. "What drives him to kill, Columbia?"

Maria smiled briefly at the nickname he had given her. "You want to understand Wyatt Butler?" she asked rhetorically. "He repairs antique watches for a living. Sells them from town to town. He's obsessed with precision. Logic. The rational flow of events. Like the ticking of a clock. It's reliable, dependable. It makes sense. It's perfect. One second comes after the other in exact movements, and so on and so on."

"Okay. What does that mean for us?"

"He plans *everything* precisely. Every move, every second is planned from beginning to end. He knew exactly where each of his victims lived, knew exactly when they'd be left home alone or when they stood outside at the bus stop. He knew how to dodge the police, and he knew how to keep a low profile, even as he went from town to town murdering children."

"So why kids?"

"Think about it. What's more chaotic than the mind and actions of a child? They're illogical decision-makers. Unorganized. They trust for no reason. They deceive for no reason. They destroy for fun. He doesn't understand them. And that's why he despises them. In his mind, they represent everything that's wrong with humanity. He feels like if he can just rid the world of that disorder, everything will be perfect and precise. And he wants to be the one to get the credit for doing it. That's important."

Butler's mind was a dark, dark place. Dredging up all these memories of him was always tough. It brought back unwanted visions of the trial. Unwanted memories of the questions people posed to her about his methods. Unwanted experiences in the deliberation room, repeatedly going through the evaluations and photographs.

But as always, the hardest part to recall was his mentality. She'd buried what she knew about his subconscious deep into her own.

"Reese, he treats everything like his watches. Calculated. Perfectly rational. He's got this all planned out. It's what makes him so deadly. And difficult to catch."

"Then how'd they catch him before?"

"Believe me, the only reason the authorities got their hands on Wyatt Butler was because he wanted them to catch him. Why? I don't know."

Reese frowned. "But they didn't catch the real killer, did they?"

Maria gazed back, unmoving. She suddenly felt like she was being interrogated. "I'm sorry," she said. "I'm not sure what you mean."

"You're the one who set Wyatt Butler free. You voted not guilty. I watched the video of your press conference. That was a brave thing to do. You didn't deserve what the press did to you afterward."

"Nobody would."

"I'm sure."

He doesn't know what it was like. The horrors of being on that jury. The aftermath that wrecked their lives.

"Here's the million-dollar question, Ms. Fontana. Am I looking for Wyatt Butler, or am I looking for someone else?"

Maria could tell he was leading her in a specific direction. Her mind raced trying to figure out his intention. It was better to stay silent and allow the officer to elaborate.

"Someone with intimate knowledge of this case," he finally added.

"Surely you can't think it's me?"

"For a brief moment, the thought had occurred to me. But clearly, you're not the one on the tape. And not only that, I recognize the look in your eyes. You're genuinely afraid of this guy, I can tell. I trust my gut, and it's saying to trust you."

"Okay, so what are you saying?" she asked. "There's something you're not telling me, Mr. Reese. What is it?"

He took in a long, slow breath. Slid the file folder across the desk. "You should know . . . this is . . . hard to look at."

Maria slowly opened the folder. Inside, a photo of Jeremy Finch's decapitated head arranged neatly on a bed stared back at her through wide, dead eyes.

A sound escaped from Maria's throat. Something between a scream and yelp. She covered her mouth with her hands to stop herself, but the image was so graphic. It was the first time she'd seen someone she knew chopped up like this. The feeling was unexpected. Somehow more shocking than any of the photos she'd seen in the courtroom.

"*Finch?*" Maria said breathlessly. "The author? *That's* who you found on the eighth floor?"

Reese nodded. "It's Finch, all right."

"Why the hell didn't you tell me this sooner?"

"I thought you might've already known. Please understand—"

"How the hell would I know? How did it even get here? Was Finch a passenger?"

"No. Whoever did this, whether it's Butler or a copycat, brought Finch's head on board with them."

"But why would he go after Finch?"

"That's my question to you, Maria. Why *would* he go after Finch? If notoriety really is one of Butler's motivators, then why would he go after the man who cemented his legacy for him? Twelve consecutive weeks on the *New York Times* Best Seller List . . ."

"I-I don't know," Maria muttered, turning her eyes away from the horrific Polaroid. "I have to think . . ."

"There might be another possibility to consider. Hear me out, Maria. Is there anyone else on this boat who has the motivation to kill Jeremy Finch?"

Maria looked back at him, finally understanding his implication. "You can't be serious. You mean Steve?"

Reese remained tight-lipped, but the look in his eye said it all.

"You think Steve did this?" Maria spat. "And you think I knew about it? Are you crazy?"

"Think this through with me. This man, Jeremy Finch. He practically ruined your life. The shitstorm that rained down on you after your press conference and his book? I can't imagine the pressure you and your family were under. You must at least acknowledge the possibility that Steve might have taken matters into his own hands."

Maria raced to process the accusation.

At the very least, she knew that she was innocent. No amount of paranoia or fear could make her question that. Even though she hated Finch about as much as she'd hated anyone, that didn't mean she'd had anything to do with his gruesome death.

But something Reese said struck a nerve with her. Something that was still nagging at the back of her mind.

"Steve might have taken matters into his own hands . . ."

She cycled through every major event between Steve and herself. Any time in the last year where she'd thought he'd acted a little odd. Sure, he was often weird and a little geeky, which was part of the reason she'd fallen in love with him. Everything was happy. Normal. Up until the day they boarded this ship.

Then, a comment from Steve, said long ago, sprang to the front of her mind. Something he'd said about Finch after they'd left the Barnes & Noble signing at Union Square.

"He'll never, ever hurt you or our family again."

Her hands tightened around the chair's arms.

No . . . no . . .

That can't be.

"I spoke to Steve, you know," Reese said. "He'd mentioned that you two met after the trial. Is that right?"

Maria thought back to the weeks after the mistrial. She was coming home late from work one night and barely missed the F train to Queens. At that time of night, she would have to wait close to an hour until the next one arrived. Steve, the only other person left on the empty platform, offered to split a cab with her, and the rest was history. In the moment, it felt like a scene out of a movie. They'd laughed in the cab. Had so much in common. Exchanged numbers.

Now that she thought back on it, Steve had somewhat appeared out of nowhere. A completely empty train station in the middle of the night. And then all of a sudden, this tall, lanky man standing right beside her.

But is Reese saying what I think he's saying?

"*Steve?* You think Steve is the copycat?"

Just the thought of it made Maria want to vomit. All the nights she'd spent in bed by his side. All the afternoon kisses and homemade meals. She twisted the ring on her finger. The smooth feel now felt calculated rather than comforting.

"He has intimate knowledge of Butler's crimes," Reese said. "He could be replicating Butler's style to shift the blame away himself. Killing Finch was personal for him. Killing the little girl was to cover his tracks."

"I don't believe what I'm hearing. It's just not possible."

"Think about it. Steve knew the second you heard the details about the severed head, you'd put two and two together and instantly suspect Butler. He was probably counting on it. He probably even knew you'd bring that information to me."

"Steve's not capable of something like that. He's not capable of any of this."

"I was a cop for a long time before this," Reese replied, looking out the window. "You'd be shocked at what people are capable of."

Maria silently shook her head.

It all seemed so inconceivable. Yet, at the same time, plausible if she stripped her emotions away from the facts. She had to admit, it was impossible to rule Steve out with absolute certainty.

And that final thought consumed her with dread.

"There are lots of weirdos out there," Reese said. "They get obsessed with these serial killer cases and try to get close to the people involved. You were the only juror to make yourself publicly known. I'm not saying he is, but if Steve was one of these people looking for an in, you would've been the best and easiest route. Single mom . . ."

Maria shut her eyes. It was something she'd never considered before. In her joy of finding a love, she never stopped to wonder if Steve's intentions were honest. Sure, at times she'd thought it had been too good to be true. But who didn't when they eventually found their ideal partner and soul mate?

She cast her mind back to their argument the previous night. About Steve leaving the room when she'd told him to stay. About his possible whereabouts while the crimes on board were committed.

No. She refused to believe it.

But . . . if there was even the slightest *chance that Reese was right . . .*

No matter how small that possibility . . .

The twins. Chloe and Christopher. They were still in the cabin with him.

Oh my God.

"My kids!" she blurted.

Maria bolted out of her chair, charged across the operations room, and flung open the door. Reese followed suit, quickly fastening his holster to his belt and bounding after her.

Tears stung Maria's eyes as she darted down the stairs to the ninth floor, desperate to protect her kids at all cost.

34

Maria sprinted through the ninth-deck corridor as fast as humanly possible. The residual pain in her hip shot up her leg with each pounding footstep. Reese ran by her side, keeping one hand over his holster. She hoped he would not need the weapon.

A security guard stood idly outside Maria's stateroom. Leaning against the wall. Headphones in. Thumbing through something on his phone. His head snapped up when Maria's and Reese's footsteps pounded toward him.

A wave of relief washed over Maria.

The startled guard pulled the headphones from his ears.

Reese and Maria finally reached the cabin door and stopped on a dime. She rested her hands on her knees and sucked in deep breaths.

"Has anyone come in or out?" Reese wheezed.

"No," the guard answered, slightly confused. "I've been here the whole time. Nothing unusual."

Maria slid her key card into the slot and flung open the door to room 925. Reese instantly forced his way past, pistol raised.

Nothing moved in the living area. Empty, but it had telltale signs of a struggle. The coffee table was pushed out of place, checkers and Jenga blocks had spilled across the carpet. The TV had a distinct crack in the display. And the minifridge was knocked off its platform, the door swinging slightly on its hinges.

"Holy shit," Reese said.

All Maria's personal belongings on the dresser now littered the floor in disarray. Nothing was in its right place.

No no no no.

"Christopher! Chloe! Steve!" Maria screamed out through the chaos. She ducked into the smaller bedroom. Empty. The bedding lied crumpled on the floor as if kicked off in a haste. She sprinted toward the master bedroom. Same thing.

Her entire family . . .

Gone.

She rushed back out into the living room. Desperately searched for any clue.

Reese held his gun at the ready up in the air, his finger by the trigger. "Where are they?" Maria cried out. "What happened?"

Something caught her eye as she raced back toward the twins' room. She stopped midstride. A flutter of white cloth moved near the wall. A white linen curtain, knocked off its rod from whatever struggle had blown through here. A gentle breeze flowed in from outside and lifted the sheet up, sending another ripple of fabric floating into the air.

The balcony door is open.

She sprinted toward the sliding door and heaved it fully open.

Then took in the scene to her front.

Maria's legs buckled. She dropped to her knees. Stared open-mouthed in utter shock.

Steve's lifeless body had been propped like a marionette against the balcony railing. Dried blood had caked his slit throat. The deep cut ran from ear to ear.

This isn't real. This isn't real.

But no amount of mental denial would usher this crushing reality away.

"*Steve!* No! *No!*"

"My God," Reese said.

Reese moved to Maria's side. Aimed to his left and right. Glanced back inside the cabin.

Maria threw herself down onto the floor and collapsed into Steve's chest. His body was rigid. Heavy. Lifeless.

She took his head in her hands. He felt cold to the touch. Almost freezing. His rosy-red cheeks had faded into a soft icy blue. She clapped her palms around his face. The blood drenched her shirt, but she didn't care.

"Please . . . ," she choked out. "Steve . . . please . . ."

Reese raised his walkie-talkie to his mouth. "Alpha. Alpha. Alpha. I need a medical team to cabin 925 immediately."

Maria knew it was only to confirm the obvious. She propped Steve's injured neck into the crook of her elbow. She brought his face close to hers. Closed his eyelids to stop his terrible dead-eyed stare.

Nothing will bring him back.

But her focus jumped back to the one thing she could still save.

The kids.

"*Christopher! Chloe!*" she yelled, more out of hope than expectation.

She sprang to her feet and headed for the smaller bedroom again. To find any signs of a clue. Any hint that the kids were still alive. Nothing.

Maria returned to the living area.

"No one came into this cabin?" Reese growled toward the entrance.

"No one. I swear!" the flustered guard shouted back.

"Then how the *fuck* did this happen?"

"I don't know. Honestly, I was outside the whole time. Not a single person came or left!"

"And you didn't hear anything?"

"I'm . . . I'm sorry," the young officer stuttered, motioning to his headphones. "I'm so sorry."

"Goddamn it! You're fucking useless."

In the bedroom, Maria dropped to her knees. Hitting the floor hard. She looked under the bed, praying for a chance her kids were hiding somewhere.

"*Chloe? Christopher?*"

Nothing. Dust sat on the carpet beneath the box spring. It kicked up and swirled in the air as Maria bolted upright.

She yanked the closet open, almost ripping the door off its hinges. It was empty. The kids' formal clothes still swayed on the hangers inside.

"*Christopher! Chloe!*" Maria yelled again.

She stomped around like a raging bull, tearing through the room blindly, searching for something she knew wasn't there. She stopped in the living room again and peered back through the sliding-glass door.

Steve's body was a sight that would be burned into her mind for the rest of her life. Stiff. Emotionless. She cringed at the sight.

She took a few tentative steps toward the balcony.

Something's missing.

Something's wrong.

"J-Jake," Maria said, barely able to catch her breath. "Jake. Tell me *exactly* what you found in the ice cream machine."

Reese stared ahead at the corpse. Stoic. Until a realization dawned on his face.

"Reese!" she bellowed, the desperation clear in her voice. "What the hell did you find?"

He spun toward her. "Two children's bathing suits."

She fought back the urge to scream.

The swimsuits had been left outside to dry yesterday.

They're gone.

Everything came together in her mind.

The twins.

He's got them.

"No! No! *No!*"

It's him.

It's Butler.

He's got my children.

"Over there," Reese said. He jabbed his finger toward the corner of the balcony.

A bloody footprint stood out against the white paint. As though whoever did this to Steve had jumped onto the railing after stepping in his blood.

Reese walked over to the railing and peered left. Then right. Then up. Then down.

"It's the balconies . . . ," he murmured aloud. "That's how he's been getting around."

Maria gazed over the rail. The huge drop to the ocean gave her butterflies. She briefly imagined Butler taking her kids on a dangerous descent, risking a plunge into the icy water.

She buckled to her knees, slumping over. Her body threatened to shut down. She squeezed her eyes shut and slapped her hands against her temples, desperately trying to wake herself up from this nightmare. But no morning sun came into view through her barely cracked eyelids. She wasn't dreaming. She was painfully awake. Painfully aware.

All this horror was real.

Steve's dead.

And my children are next.

This is it. This is the end.

Butler's reached his final act.

A trill resonated through Maria's body.

The cabin's telephone. The object that just less than an hour ago, Steve had held high above his head as a weapon when they first entered the room during the ship-wide lockdown. Protecting her. Protecting the kids. Maria's heart ached to think that in the last moments he'd spent alive, she had spent them doubting him, even in the slightest.

The phone sat on a ledge by the front door, untouched by the previous disturbance and her frantic search.

It rang in loud blasts.

BRRRING!

BRRRING!

Reese looked toward the phone and then back at Maria. His eyes communicated a clear message: *Don't answer. Don't do it.*

The phone rang on, unhindered by his caution.

BRRRING!

Fighting back tears, Maria marched past Reese. Pushed past the stunned guard and stood by the phone. She slammed her finger down on the Speaker button and tensed up, sealing in the tiny pockets of air her sobbing lungs barely clung to.

The receiver clicked. The sound of heavy breathing sizzled through the phone's speaker. After a few seconds, a voice finally crackled in.

"*Hello, Maria.*" The voice took a brief pause. The room around her went spinning. Dizzy. Upside down.

"*I'm sure by now you realize who this is . . .*"

35

Maria stood paralyzed to the spot. She instantly recognized the voice of Wyatt Butler. A fact she'd suspected, yet dreaded, and one that nobody could now ignore. *"Now, shall we discuss your children?"* Butler asked.

He sounded exactly the way she remembered him. Smug. Arrogant. A harsh Brooklyn accent topped with that infuriating tone of nonchalance.

This time, it wasn't someone else's family he'd hurt. It was her own. She stood there. Frozen. On the verge of collapse.

The stillness that filled the room lasted a moment too long.

Say something, damn it.

Maria went to speak, though only produced a silent stutter.

In an instant, images from the trial flooded her mind. The hideous contours of dead children. Her own children's faces taking their place in the next macabre installment.

"I have them here with me," Butler bragged. *"In my cabin."*

"Chloe! Christopher!" she shouted into the speaker. "I'm here! Mom's here!"

Nobody replied. Not even a single sound to betray the presence of her kids on the other end of the phone.

A bead of sweat trickled down her back.

She balled her fists to stop her hands from trembling.

"They can't hear you," Butler said. Joyously. Obnoxiously.

"Put them on the phone," Maria demanded. "Right now."

More silence followed. Painful and long. She feared hearing one of the twins scream. Or some other depraved act carried out by Butler.

Reese stepped closer to her. Closer to the phone.

Finally, a tiny chuckle slipped out of the speaker. Butler unable to contain his delight. The same dismissive laugh that echoed around the quiet courtroom when the prosecution had attempted to link him to every murder.

"You'd like to speak with them?" Butler asked, drawing out her desperation.

The panic inside Maria began to fuse with her rage.

He's toying with me.

She clenched her teeth together and pushed out the next word. As though she were reading his script. "Yes."

Butler pulled the receiver closer to his mouth, causing his voice to reverberate even more.

"I must warn you, Maria . . . ," he whispered. *"They're* very *scared . . ."*

It sounded like footsteps crossing a room.

A door opening.

"Mommy! *Mommy!*" Chloe yelled.

"*Mommy!*" Christopher shouted. "Please come get us. He's hurting us."

The kids shouted at the same time, blocking each other out.

Blocking out any potential clues.

Maria shut her eyes. Tried to think of a way around this. Anything to put her on the front foot against Butler before he killed her two main reasons for living.

In an instant, the twins' shouts stopped.

Maria shut her eyes. Tears poured down her face as her cheeks rose to meet them. One hand shot up to her chest and clutched at the bundle of fabric above her sternum, smearing herself in more of Steve's blood. She clasped her other hand over her mouth, trying to conceal the sobs on the brink of erupting out.

Butler's skin-crawling breaths echoed through the speaker.

"I'm giving you the chance to see them again, Maria. Would you like that?"

"Where are you?" Reese shouted. "Butler? What cabin are you in?"

Unsurprisingly, Butler stayed silent.

Just his rhythmic breaths came through the speaker.

"Butler? Where are you?" Reese urged.

Nothing.

More crackling breaths.

In and out.

In and out.

Maria told herself to get it together.

He only wants to talk to me.

"Where should I go?" she asked, beginning to regain her composure.

"You should know how to find me . . . ," Butler said, pausing.

Reese looked at Maria with confusion before Butler finished his thought.

"Considering we've already met."

His last sentence had slipped into a drawl. The familiar Southern accent she'd heard earlier in the day. Only hours ago.

The elderly woman.

Her caretaker.

Maria cast her mind back to standing in line at the coffee shop earlier that day. Down by her side, the friendly wrinkled face of Catherine Davies smiled up from her wheelchair. And then the old woman's words:

The caretaker that deserved a nice vacation.

The caretaker who'd had all those surgeries.

Maria tried to pull the man's face back from her memory. Tall, lanky even. Unfashionable yet functional clothing. A thin, handsome face. A five-o'clock shadow outlined his square jaw.

His eyes.

They were a deep, chocolate brown. As dark as the coffee he'd held in his hand. During the trial, Butler's natural eye color was on display. A sickly mixture of amber and green.

They must've been contacts.

The old lady's words kept running through her head.

All the surgeries he's been through the past two years . . .

I should have known.

A shiver shot through her spine. She shuddered at being so close to him.

In the restaurant.

He'd been within touching distance.

Inches away.

Inches away from my kids.

Steve had even helped him, moving chairs out of his way so Catherine could get to a table. Bile rose in Maria's throat. She looked out toward the balcony. Toward her fiancé's corpse. The blood from his neck had begun to dry and congeal, leaving sticky carmine blotches splattered across his clothes.

"But you'll need to come soon."

Butler's voice snapped Maria's gaze back toward the phone.

"In five minutes, I'm going to throw them over the railing on my balcony. The Atlantic looks rough today, Maria. Rougher than the other night . . ."

"Don't you *fucking* touch them!" Maria roared. A swell of fury pushed the tears from her eyes and replaced them with a cold hatred.

Even through the phone, she could hear the twins in the background start to scream in response to Butler's admission.

"Shhh-sh-sh." The deranged man's poor attempt at calming the kids.

He pulled the phone back up to his ear. *"The children make too much noise, Maria. I'm not sure how long I can wait . . ."* Butler's voice trailed off.

Maria wanted to scream at him. To rip the phone out of the wall and smash it against the ground. Her hands curled into fists as she imagined tearing his eyes from their sockets and spitting on his corpse.

It was a pure rage. A feeling she'd never experienced. A demon she didn't know she had inside her.

Reese's hand wrapped around her wrist, pulling her back to Earth's gravity. She looked up at him through her rigid scowl. Reese's eyes were wide. Yet still. Calmer than hers.

I can't lose it.

I have to stay calm.

As calm as Butler.

"You have exactly five minutes to get here," Butler reminded.

"You must come alone. Five minutes to see your children. To see them in their last moments of life."

He took another breath. A sigh, almost.

"They would really like to see you, Maria. They've been asking for you."

Maria had seconds to think.

This is it. My only chance.

I need to outthink him.

I need to change the rules of his game.

I need to break him.

"Maria?" Butler said in a singsong voice. *"Are you still there, Maria?"*

He needs precision.

He needs order.

He needs everything to go according to his plan.

The way it already has been this entire time.

She looked up at Reese. He looked back at her with a questioning brow. His neck tilted forward in Maria's direction. Prodding. Waiting for her to make a move.

"Yes," she finally choked out. "Thank you for letting me know, Wyatt."

Reese looked at her in surprise. He would understand soon.

Maria took a deep breath in through her nostrils, mustering up the strength for what she was about to say. What she was about to do.

She leaned in toward the phone and spoke.

"I'm not coming."

She slammed her finger down on the receiver, ending the call.

Hanging up on Wyatt Butler.

Hanging up on her children.

36

Reese stood staring in disbelief. He couldn't comprehend what he'd just seen. The terrifying sequence of events on board had quickly escalated, but Maria's decision had topped everything.

"What the hell are you doing?" he asked.

"Don't you see? He *wants* me to go to him. It's part of his plan."

"What about your kids?" Reese fired back. "What about them?"

"It's a trap. It has to be. If I go to him, he'll kill them. The only chance we've got is to act illogically. Break his plan."

Her instincts seemed so counterintuitive.

She's abandoning her own children.

Leaving them to die with that madman.

"We're wasting time," Reese said. "He gave you five minutes."

"Five minutes is the time he's given himself if everything goes according to his plan. But we're not proceeding according to his plan. His timeframe is not ours. We have to make time stop. He wants everything to run perfectly. Like one of his fucking antique watches. We can't give that to him."

"Maria, please," Reese implored. "I don't follow."

"Time must run out."

"Then how do we get to the kids?" Hendricks added.

"*We* don't get to the kids. *You* do." She stared at both of the officers. "He wants me to watch them die. If I go, they're as good as gone. He won't do anything until I'm there to watch."

Reese half shrugged, unsure of how to proceed. "We don't even know what room they're in—"

"Look on the manifest for a passenger named Catherine Davies. Find her and we find Butler's cabin."

"Catherine Davies? Who the hell is that?"

"A sick old woman. Butler's been posing as her caretaker. He changed his appearance. Changed his voice."

"How do you know?"

"Because I met him earlier this morning."

"You've already come face-to-face with him?"

"He's unrecognizable. But it's him. Find that room and you'll find Wyatt Butler."

Reese considered if Maria was losing it.

She just lost her fiancé. She's still covered in his blood.

Her children are in mortal danger.

Should she really be the one making decisions?

Hendricks looked at him to make the next move. Reese took a moment to think, considering the facts at hand.

But she's been right about Butler all along.

Now we're running out of time.

Maybe this is our only option.

Reese nodded toward Hendricks.

She instantly reacted, clicking the Transmit button on her walkie-talkie. "St. Clair. Come in."

"Go for St. Clair."

"I need a search on the passenger manifest. A Catherine Davies."

Hendricks's voice trailed off as she walked farther away.

Something nudged against Reese's elbow.

"Reese," Maria said, "do you have a master key card? Something that could open any door on the ship?"

He stuffed his hand inside his jacket, feeling around for the inner pocket. Eventually, he patted down on the outline of a stiff plastic rectangle. "Yes," Reese said. "Why?"

"I need you to give it to me."

Reese eyed her with uncertainty. Maria looked like a mess. Covered in dried spatters of blood. Her curly hair pulled in every direction. Even her face looked different from the night he'd first met her in his office. Bags under her eyes. A shallowness to her cheeks. And that was just from the last few days.

Hendricks joined back into their huddle. “Maria’s right. There is a Catherine Davies on board. In room 703. Traveling with a man named Todd Ullman.”

“That’s him. That’s Butler. He’s completely changed his appearance.”

The master of disguise.

All the case files were right.

“So,” Hendricks said, “we’ve got the room number, but it’s on the other side of the ship. What’s the plan here?”

“Listen to me,” Maria ordered, “and listen carefully. Hendricks, in twenty minutes, go to that room. But it has to be twenty minutes. Exactly twenty minutes. No sooner. Go in and grab my kids, okay?”

Reese frowned. “Won’t Butler be in there with them?”

“I don’t think so. I’ll lure him out of the room before then. He’ll follow. His plan does not work without me. Reese, I’ll need the key card to get into the lower decks of the ship. That’s where we’ll take him. No balconies to climb. No railings to jump off. I don’t want him escaping. I need you to come down with me. We’ll trap him down there.”

She turned to Hendricks. “You get my children out safely. You understand me? I don’t care if I die. You still get my kids out safely. Understand?”

Hendricks agreed with a sharp nod. Something told Reese that regardless of what Butler had planned, Maria's wrath would be a thousand times worse if any harm came to her children.

"I'll be the one to draw him out," Maria repeated to herself.

"Who's to say he won't kill the kids before he leaves the room?" Reese said.

"He won't," Maria shot back. "I'd bet everything on it."

"You *are* betting everything on it."

Maria took a deep breath, the words settling into her as a hard truth. "Exactly. That's how sure I am. If this doesn't work, I'll only have myself to blame."

Reese sharply exhaled.

And I'll have two more dead kids on my hands.

37

Butler stood on the balcony of cabin 703, tightening his grip around the slim ankle in his left hand. On the other side of the safety railing, the little girl's hair swayed in the breeze. Her face reddened by the second, transforming to the color of cherry wine.

The blood rushing to her head.

He held her there. Dangling. Enjoying his own strength. And the fact that he had a life in his grip, swinging gently, upside down, over the 150-foot drop. All he had to do was part his fingers and enjoy the show.

Butler was ready to let go the moment Maria walked through the door. The minute she set eyes on him, and the realization dawned on her that she had made a mistake.

Any moment now . . .

The completion of my latest work will be spectacular.

Just inside the cabin, the Fontana boy sat slumped in a pile on the floor. Unconscious with a large lump on his forehead. Taking shallow breaths. As motionless as his sister. After their outburst on the phone, Butler knew the two of them no longer had the privilege to remain awake. They were too loud. Too risky. Too unpredictable. He didn't want any nosy, prying passengers in nearby cabins getting involved. That would mean a deviation from his plan. He'd knocked the kids out to be sure no more disturbances would interfere with his final act. His magnum opus.

My masterpiece.

He examined the children. They were supposedly twins. But Butler didn't see the resemblance. Just two blank faces. Two blights on the world, repeatedly creating a mess. When he'd entered their cabin, both had been throwing play items around the floor.

Two rats.

Lucky to even play a part in this.

A twinge of fatigue swelled through his extended arm. A reminder of how long he'd been holding this girl over the railing.

Waiting.

Waiting for Maria.

Waiting to drink in the look on her face as she watched

her daughter plummet into the icy ocean. The ultimate thrill of watching part of a mother die inside as her offspring died in front of her eyes.

Where is *she?*

Butler glanced down at the watch. A 1962 Benrus. One he'd salvaged and repaired from the brink of scrap. His finest work, if he had to say. The micron gold electroplated case had been badly mistreated by its previous owner. Neglected out of sheer stupidity. But after hours of painstaking restoration, winding, and a new quartz crystal, she ran like magic.

The watch ticked by on his wrist in pulsating beats. His flesh quivered with each click of the delicate second hand.

11:59 and twenty-two seconds.

11:59 and twenty-three seconds.

11:59 and twenty-four seconds.

His stomach churned. Her delay was beginning to nauseate him. The disorder he hated so much had started to surface again, hurtling into his consciousness.

Thirty-six more seconds.

Her final chance to see her children.

Her final chance to understand.

He peered inside the cabin toward the stateroom door, desperate not to miss the moment of Maria's arrival. Her frantic search. The horror spreading across her face. Her bloodcurdling scream would feel better than anything he had ever experienced before.

These events, carefully planned for months and years, always had one brilliant culmination that made them so unique and satisfying.

Near the kitchenette, Catherine Davies's corpse sat slumped in her wheelchair. The purple abrasions and grip marks on her neck were still fresh. Rivers of maroon and violet wrapped around her throat, melting into the creases and wrinkles she already had. A tiny cut where one of Butler's fingernails dug in a touch too deep dribbled a single droplet of blood.

This was an unfortunate consequence. The bruises were reasonably symmetrical. He accepted that they'd never form in identical shapes. But the tiny cut stood out for its lack of conformity. He grimaced.

She was no longer needed.

It hadn't taken long for Catherine to die. After disconnecting her oxygen tank, Mother Nature might have eventually finished the job had Butler not intervened sooner. With Catherine's sickly state, what normally took him a few minutes only took him fifteen seconds of forceful squeezing.

She even let out one hoarse scream near the end. Maybe the adrenaline surging around her body, desperately attempting to keep her alive. Then nothing. She didn't fight back. Instead, she just stared ahead. Straight into his eyes. Unreactive. Passive.

Probably thankful to die.

Free of her obsolete shell.

It was her time.

She'd played her part.

Butler glared at his watch again. It sneered back at him. The minute hand snapped upright, perfectly concealing the hour hand behind it.

12:00 and one second.

12:00 and two seconds.

12:00 and three seconds.

She's late.

A throbbing started at the base of his head, oozing down into his shoulder blades. None of this made sense.

She's sentenced them to death.

Sentenced them to die when she couldn't sentence me?

He looked at the little girl hanging like a pendulum from his hand. Then to the boy on the floor. Both looked like they were sleeping without a care in the world. Unaware that their mother seemingly wanted them dead.

They should already be dead.

The muscles in his left hand twitched. Each fiber wanted to drop her. Wanted to watch this little girl smack against the surface of the ocean like a water balloon on concrete.

I can't. Not yet. She needs to be here.

She needs to witness. To learn her mistake.

12:00 and fourteen seconds.

12:00 and fifteen seconds.

12:00 and sixteen seconds.

The watch's metal strap suddenly felt ice cold on his wrist.

He peered down. The second hand had stopped. Suspended in a strange matrix. Then the hour hand began to warp. Bending into winding, zigzagging shapes beneath the glass lens. Like a living Salvador Dalí painting.

Moving forward and back.

Forward and back.

The watch is mocking me.

Mocking me for believing she'd come.

Mocking me for trusting her to make the rational decision. The only *decision.*

Rage burned inside him. A heavy heat rose from his feet and filled him up to his lungs. He slammed his wrist down hard onto the railing, shattering the watch face into a mess of loose parts and glass.

What else would I expect?

From someone so illogical.

A woman who would let me go free.

He looked inside toward the stateroom door.

Waiting.

Waiting.

Still waiting.

The twinge of exhaustion in his arm had developed into a spasm. Holding the girl like this, she began to feel heavy.

He looked back down at the fragmented pieces of the Benrus that poked into his wrist.

She's not coming.

Refusing to witness her divine error.

His eyes took a slow blink out across the sea. The breathing in his nostrils intensified. Beads of sweat that had collected along his hairline now crawled into his eyelids.

She's supposed to be here.

She's supposed to be here!

"*Where is she?*" he shouted at the unconscious girl in his hand.

He turned to the bathroom, yelling toward Catherine's colorless corpse.

"*Where is she?*" he repeated aloud to no one that could hear him.

With one heaving pull, he yanked the girl back over the railing and tossed her into the corner beside the bed with her brother. Their two miniature bodies folded into one another. Their limbs pretzeled in a heap.

Butler rubbed his left biceps. The soreness was beginning to take hold. He knelt beside the unconscious twins and brought his voice down to a nearly inaudible volume.

"What kind of mother leaves her children to die?" he muttered, blinking hard.

He reached down with both hands, brushing a strand of the little girl's tangled hair behind her ear and fixing the boy's hair.

"I would leave you to die too," he said, still brushing. "But first, your mother has to understand what she's done to me."

He straightened his knees and stood upright.

"She'll pay with her own life."

She is as hopeless as a child. Illogical. Chaotic.

She cannot be taught.

She has to die.

38

Maria clambered down the stairs toward the seventh floor, the soles of her shoes barely digging into the strands of the stiff teal carpet below. She tried to stay perfectly silent. As hushed as her surroundings. The ship was sinisterly quiet in lockdown. Eerie. Each door in every direction along the corridor had been closed. Not another soul in sight. Not even a security officer. Hallways that, just an hour ago, were flooded with panic-struck passengers charging to their rooms were now deserted. Littered with the debris from their wake.

Thousands of passengers, uncertain and afraid, silently locked away in their rooms awaiting further instructions. The only sound was the crash of the ocean above the hum of the air-conditioning.

She tiptoed delicately around the dropped bags of chips, water cups, and sunglasses that littered the floor. Anything that could make a crunch. Anything that would betray her presence to Butler if he were waiting around a corner.

Reese followed alongside her. Making his way just as carefully. Gun extended.

They needed to cross over to the port side to reach Butler. They cautiously proceeded past the elevator bay and turned down the hallway that pointed toward cabins 701–749.

The tight corridor felt claustrophobic. Like the walls had closed in even farther since lockdown, denying Reese and her any extra space.

My kids are here.

In one of these rooms.

Reese held his gun down by his waist. He extended an arm out across Maria's torso, wordlessly instructing her to stop. He shuffled in front of her and took the lead, pistol at the ready, crouching low as they walked past room after room, watching the cabin numbers decrease as they made it farther and farther toward the stern of the ship.

711.

709.

707.

They hugged the wall as they came upon Catherine Davies's cabin.

703.

The brightly colored placard looked just like the hundreds of others on the ship. Gold embossed lettering just like the rest. From outer appearances, nothing out of the ordinary. Just like the room's inhabitants.

Maria had to fight off the urge to press her ear up against the door. She desperately wanted to hear even the slightest hint of her children's voices. The tiniest sign that they were still alive.

But I can't. I can't.

That's not why we're here.

She scanned the walls of the corridor.

There.

Across the hall and three doors down from Butler's cabin, Maria saw what she'd been looking for. Nestled between cabins 708 and 710 on the even side of the hallway, a smaller lightweight door sat unmarked. No numbered placard or intricate designs on the exterior. Just a plain light gray door.

A crew door.

She silently swiped the master key card into the adjoining slot and propped the door open by wedging an old room service tray in the frame.

The door jutted out into the hallway at an awkward angle. Even to Maria, it looked strange. Out of place. The only door on the entire deck that was open.

Perfect in its imperfection.

Perfect to drive Butler crazy.

Reese looked toward her with squinted eyes. Seemingly confused by her latest move. Silently, she motioned for him to step inside. He looked back at the door to cabin 703. They were so close. Just a few feet away from where her children were being held captive. One kicked-in door and a well-placed bullet away from saving Christopher's and Chloe's lives.

Maria felt it too. The overwhelming screams of her instincts begging to charge into that room were difficult to ignore. But for this plan to work, she couldn't see them. Couldn't even call through the door to let them know she hadn't abandoned them.

I have to let Butler's time run out on him.

He has to believe I am not coming.

That's Chloe and Christopher's only chance.

She and Reese ducked beneath the crew door into the even tighter passageway that led to the inner facilities and service areas of the ship.

This entire service corridor was neat and tidy. Everything had a place, perfectly positioned, secured to specific spots on the boat. Room service carts, giant supply bins, brand-new mattresses wrapped in plastic. Everything stored in ninety-degree angles, everything positioned to maximize precious space.

Maria knew Butler would love the preciseness and perfection of this hallway.

So, as they quickened their pace down the corridor, Maria flung open every door she could. Pushed every cart out of place. Tipped over everything she could wrangle free. Hoping it would plunge Butler's mind into chaos.

I need to unnerve him. Provoke him.

Get him to make uncalculated decisions.

Maria flung open the door to one of the many laundry rooms on the ship. Huge industrial washing machines still chugged along inside, tumbling pounds of bedsheets and towels as if the happy voyage of days ago was still underway. She yanked open one of the washing machine doors, reached in, and pulled out a wad of sopping-wet tablecloths. With one big toss, she launched the dripping fabrics across the floor.

"What are you doing?" Reese asked, looking disturbed by her actions.

"Bait," Maria explained. "This is how we'll lure him down here. He won't be able to handle it. The purposeless chaos. The disorder I'm causing. It'll send him into a rage. And that's when he'll realize he's trapped."

"A rage? Is that what we want? A psychopathic killer pushed into even more anger?" Reese shrugged and looked down at the screen of his cell phone. "It's been twenty minutes. Hendricks should be at the cabin by now."

Shit.

Butler might already be in this corridor following us.

"We've gotta move. Hurry!"

Maria took off running. The farther away she could lure

Butler from her kids, the better. The more time it gave Hendricks and security to enter the cabin and rescue Chloe and Christopher. It was on their shoulders to get the twins out safe. Maria couldn't bear to imagine the alternative.

Reese hustled to keep up. Maria opened one last door before taking a sharp left. She darted around the corner, nearly clipping the same injured hip she'd already slammed against the edge of the wall. She looked over her shoulder as she ran, waiting for Reese to catch up.

A dense crack rang out through the corridor, echoing off every piece of steel and metal frame of each open door.

Maria stopped dead in her tracks. Silently, she tiptoed back to the intersection where she'd turned. She peered around the corner.

Reese's limp body was splayed across the tiled floor. Unconscious. Blood oozed from a laceration on his upper forehead.

Above him, a tall, lanky figure stood below the harsh fluorescent lights, his bony knuckles gripped around a heavy pipe.

Maria's hand shot up to her mouth, smothering the sharp gasp that rocketed from her throat.

Butler.

He sussed out the trap.

Wyatt Butler loomed over Reese like an unhinged demon. He was covered in blood. Probably Steve's. He drew in dense, hulking wheezes. Almost asthmatic. The Southern charm from his time as Todd Ullman had been completely replaced by the most sadistic version of his true self. The version many unfortunate children witnessed before taking their final breaths.

She prayed Chloe and Christopher had not taken theirs.

Despite setting this trap, the sight of Butler had paralyzed her. Tears streamed down her cheeks. In a panic, she reached around into her pockets and ripped out the master key card. She turned to the closest door on her left, swiped the key card, and flung it open.

A stairwell.

Going down.

Deeper into the bowels of the ship.

She gawked at the stairs, frozen. Until the sounds of footsteps running full force at her knocked her back into motion. She grabbed the handrail and dashed inside the landing.

Butler immediately followed. His footsteps drew closer every second.

She grabbed the door handle behind her and slammed it shut.

BANG!

Butler flung his body into the door just as it latched shut. He rattled the handle violently, unable to get in without a key.

Maria didn't stop to think. She bolted down the stairs. As

she rounded the landing for the next flight down, she glanced back up.

Wyatt Butler stared through the door's porthole window. The dimples by his mouth curled into a putrid smile. He lifted a blood-covered hand into view of the window and twiddled his fingers.

An ungodly wave in her direction.

Maria ducked and sprinted down the stairwell.

He can't get in this way. Not without a master key card.

I'm safe. I'm safe. I'm safe.

The thought repeated itself in her head over and over again. Trying to convince herself.

But she knew the truth.

Butler would not be stopped.

She was in the chase for her very life.

39

Butler watched through the door window as Maria Fontana sprinted down the stairs and disappeared onto the deck below. He waited there a few extra moments, staring at the empty stairwell.

He turned away from the locked door and stared at the opposite wall.

She's ruined my plans.

Again.

Again, she's made the wrong decision.

Maria Fontana had never learned from her mistakes. Never understood that the world should have a perfect order. And anyone who strove to create this had always come out on top.

Butler stepped forward until his face was up against the cool white metal of the paneled wall. He pressed his forehead against it. Hard. The buzzing in his head refused to stop. A shudder blew through his jaw and rattled his teeth.

He paced back and forth in the hallway. The corridor Maria had thrown into chaos. He could feel the blood pulsing in his temples. His thoughts grew dizzy. The disorder caused him physical pain. He would take this moment of stress out of her with ten times the force. Make the death of her kids even more painful than his original, merciful idea of dropping them off the balcony.

The Fontana kids would have their own tableaus on the ship. He would make sure of it.

My plan was perfect.

Everything was perfect.

And she *ruined it.*

Why wouldn't she come save her children? Why can't she understand what I've done? What I'm doing.

He glanced around him. The hallway was in complete disarray. Doors swung open along both sides in a random pattern. Chunks of laundry and scuffed footprints covered the unglazed mosaic tile floor.

Butler felt the neurons in his brain firing on top of each other. A shooting migraine rocked toward the front of his skull. He gripped at his temples as the thoughts in his head screamed at him as he paced back and forth, back and forth.

She's hiding from me. She can't hide forever. There's nowhere for her to go. She's still here. On the ship. I'll find her. I have to. If I don't stop her, who will? She's a menace. A living nightmare. I can't allow her to live. Not the way she is. I gave her a chance to learn. She's unable to learn. She'll have to come back. Yes. She'll need to go back. Eventually, she'll need to retrieve her kids. I'll go back to the cabin. Wait for her there. No. No. Security is likely there already. I'll wait outside her room. Wait for her to get her lover's body. No. I'll wait here. No. No! *No more waiting. I don't wait for her. She must come to me. She must be the one. To come to me groveling on her knees. Willing to learn. Begging to change. She's robbed me. She owes me that much. The doors are locked. Nothing is in order. I cannot think. I need to get somewhere else. Somewhere without this chaos.*

Butler took off down the straightaway. Maria had caused total carnage with everything behind him. He needed to go forward. Advance out of this madness. Butler turned to the left. Then to the right. Left. Then right. Winding through the extensive labyrinthine system that made up the crew's quarters.

"Can I help you, sir?"

A man's voice echoed from down the hall. From another intersecting corridor to his right. Butler didn't turn at the sound.

"Sir, no one is allowed to be moving around the ship. We're on a security lockdown, even the crew."

Butler stayed perfectly still, listening to each footstep as the man shuffled toward him. "Then why are you here?" he asked, without turning around.

"I am the floor monitor. Sir, I need to escort you back to your cabin."

Closer.

"Excuse me? Sir?"

Closer.

The crewmember approached him from behind, reaching out to tap him on the shoulder. "I'm sorry, sir, but you'll need to come with—"

Butler slowly turned on his heels. For a millisecond, the crewmember's mouth opened in shock as he caught sight of the blood-spattered shirt.

In the blink of an eye, Butler grabbed both sides of his head and twisted it with tremendous force, breaking his neck. A dull crack echoed through the corridor.

The man collapsed by Butler's shoes.

Butler jammed his hand into the man's pocket, feeling around with the dexterous tips of his fingers. His ring finger edged along the side of a stiff rectangle.

Yes.

He pulled the master key card out and examined it. A simple card. Blank and white with a black magnetic strip on the back. He tested it out, sliding it into one of the access-only doors behind him. The tiny LED bulb on the card swipe switched from red to green.

The chaos in his mind finally began to settle as he turned back toward the stairwell.

She couldn't have gone very far.

40

Maria's heart hammered against her chest. Her lungs burned like two hot coals. She hadn't run this fast in a long time. Certainly not since having the twins. For an instant, her mind flashed back to all the cold New York mornings arriving at Columbia's campus, watching the university's cross-country team running by through the snow of Morningside Park. She pitied them then. Empathized even more now.

She raced through empty corridor after empty corridor, no crew anywhere in sight, descending farther down into the bowels of the ship. With the entire vessel on lockdown, she had to assume help wasn't arriving. She had to assume she was on her own.

Maria continued to drive forward, sucking in deep breaths. She flinched every few seconds, half expecting Butler to yank her back by her hair or tackle her to the ground. At any moment, he could appear.

And when their paths crossed, and they would, he'd try everything to destroy her. Eviscerate her. Drain her of every last drop of blood in her veins. Just like he did to all those children. If he caught her, Maria knew the death that followed would not be a quick one. Whatever drove a man to devise a murderous rampage two years in the making, the climax he'd imagined for himself was sure to be extravagant. Bloody. Painful.

The thought of it pushed her legs even faster.

He was after *her.*

But why?

She rushed down a flight of stairs, then skidded to a stop, gazing down a massive, wide-open corridor with steel walls painted light blue. Printed arrows on the ground divided each side of the hallway, diverting foot traffic. She suddenly realized where she was.

Deck Zero. Where the crew moves beneath our feet.

What did Reese call it?

The Highway.

She took a few steps out onto the long expanse of concrete floor. A low-pitched, humming buzz rumbled down here. The air felt closer. Warmer. Enveloping her clammy skin. Nowhere near the comfortable, cool level the passengers enjoyed on the higher decks.

Maria visually searched the gloomy doorways. Not a single person in sight. No dining workers carrying platters of food. No butlers, laundry attendants, or customer service staff flitting about to their next station.

Just her.

Just emptiness.

A new sound broke through the thrumming.

In the distance, from the stairwell behind her, footsteps hammered down.

Someone racing toward her. Chasing her down. Growing louder by the second. Wyatt Butler, and he'd be here in seconds.

Fuck.

She sprinted to the nearest door.

Bright yellow letters had been painted on in a military font.

Engine Room. Door 1.

She slid her key card into the slot. A beep sounded, and the pinhead light flicked to green. The mechanism in the door whirred, and a heartbeat later, the lock thudded open. She peered back down the hallway. Butler hadn't burst into the Highway just yet.

Maria gripped the locking wheel and heaved it counterclockwise, in the direction of the stenciled letter *O*.

It took all her strength to complete a revolution, but she continued to turn, using every ounce of energy. Eventually, the wheel loosened to a fast spin for a couple of seconds, then abruptly stopped. She hauled open the door. Slipped through the gap without looking back. Closed it behind her, unaware if Butler had appeared and caught a fleeting sight of her.

Maria closed the door. Her auditory senses were immediately knocked out. The deafening whirring from the engine filled the air. The source of the hum she'd heard from the Highway, only twenty times louder. The source of the steady vibration that ran through every deck of the ship. She looked up toward the ceiling. Four decks high to house the massive, thrumming engine.

Enormous fuel pumps sent gallons of diesel through the entire system. Exhaust manifolds shot steaming hot air out of each gasket. It was a miraculous sight. A complicated puzzle of mechanical components that all rotated and churned in perfect synchronicity. But this wasn't the time for a tour.

Maria sprinted around the corner, past a wall of switchboards, and barreled into someone in the aisle.

She tripped. Her shoulder crashed into the ground, hard. Her hands scraped against the untreated concrete floor, ripping skin from her palms and fingers.

"Jeez! Watch where you're going!"

Maria scrambled to her feet. Backed away until she realized it was a crewmember.

By the looks of it, an engineer, dressed in a fluorescent-green high-vis jacket and a hard hat. He had a plump, round face. Unsmiling. Definitely unaware of the trouble that was almost certainly heading their way.

The engineer dusted himself off and gave Maria a look of curiosity, realizing she wasn't anyone he recognized or who should have had access to the engine room. A civilian. A passenger.

"Hey! You're not allowed to be down here!" he shouted toward her over the roar of the engine.

Maria motioned for him to run. Before he responded, she turned and headed off. Kept swerving to avoid the chained-off areas. Grabbed the rail to help her round corners faster. She glanced over her shoulder for a second.

"*Hey!*" the engineer called after her.

She ran a few more yards and ducked beneath a low-hanging support beam.

A loud crack rose above the sound of the engine.

Maria peered back in the direction of the engineer, fearing the worst.

And the worst had appeared.

Butler stood over cut the engineer's prone body. Wrench lazily hanging from his right hand. He stared at her. Slowly rose a finger in her direction.

"No," she gasped.

The engineer groggily grabbed Butler's leg.

Butler stomped on his face. Hard and fast, making the back of the man's head batter the ground. Then he leaned down and rammed the wrench into the engineer's throat. Twisted while forcing it down with increasing force. Blood sprayed from a wound, giving Butler's T-shirt a fresh coat. But he didn't seem to care. He turned toward Maria with a blank expression, like he'd just put together a piece of furniture. Maria thrust away from the beam. Huge fuel-purifying tanks surrounded her on both sides of the walkway. They whirred together like one gigantic vacuum. But this way had led to a dead end.

She'd had accidentally blocked herself in.

Oh shit.

She turned on a dime and bolted back, trying to find an alternative route before Butler gave chase. Just as she reached the corner, Butler appeared from behind a machine. Inches from her face. Closing off her escape route.

Maria lurched away. Her back hammered against the metal rail. She went to run to her left.

Butler anticipated the move and stepped in that direction.

She went to run to her right.

He stepped across her path again.

Maria turned toward him. There was no way out.

Butler glared at her with a look of utter contempt.

Almost his entire body had been spattered with blood. Steve's, Reese's, the engineer's, and God knows who else's. It made him appear even more chilling than normal. Nothing, seemingly, was going to stop his rampage.

An overhead floodlight blazed down on the two of them,

allowing Maria a closer look at what Wyatt Butler had become to achieve his plan.

He'd completely transformed himself. His entire face. Unrecognizable from the man she watched in the courtroom two years prior. A fuller jaw outlined the corners above his neck. His hairline had been pushed back. A nose job shaved down the pronounced bridge he'd sported at the trial. He'd lost weight too. The bulk of muscle he'd put on during his time held at Rikers had all but melted away.

He's been hiding in plain sight.

This is why the police sketches never matched.

Why none of the witnesses could ever identify him.

He lunged a step forward. Closer. She could feel his steady breaths against her face.

"Ms. Fontana, finally." His voice pitched up two octaves. "Hello, my darlin' . . ."

In an instant, he slipped back into that Southern accent he'd used to get so close to her on the pool deck. Then his voice dropped deeper.

"How have you been, dear?"

And just like that, his accent had a thick English intonation.

Maria stood motionless. Pinned into the corner like a trapped mouse by this chameleon.

"Have you thought about me?" he asked, rotating somewhere between French and German.

Maria fought back a scream. A call for help would be useless in the engine room anyway.

She opened her mouth to speak. The words barely leached out.

"You're not . . . *you*."

Butler grinned, revealing a set of bloodstained teeth. He dropped his voice back down. His timbre and heavy New York accent from the trial returned instantly. "Oh, but I am."

He took another step closer.

"You see, it's a lesson I learned early on in my life. Changing the face of a watch is easy. Changing the movements within is much more difficult."

A shudder ran through Maria's body. It could have been from the rail or a reaction of this monster to her front, looking as if he were now enjoying this moment. For him, perhaps, a moment of triumph.

"But *you* haven't changed at all, have you?" Butler hissed.

He took a step closer.

"You're just as I remember you. Sitting in that jury box. Uncertain. Sick."

He examined her for a moment. "Disgusted by the magnificence laid out before you. I can tell you feel the same now. Nothing's changed for you."

Maria sucked in a sharp breath. "This is all about me, isn't it?" she asked.

"Very good, Professor Fontana," he replied. "Finally, you're learning. The last two years of my life are very much about you. You and that defective mind of yours."

"Then why kill Finch? Why kill those children? They have nothing to do with me."

He smiled. Smug. Full of himself.

"Why, I thought you'd enjoy me separating Jeremy Finch's head from his body. You know, I read that book he wrote. He wasn't very nice toward you, was he? Or your family. I assume you received the copy I left in your mailbox?"

It was Butler.

He was the one who'd written "You were wrong" *in that book . . .*

Maria stayed silent, trying to piece Butler's plan together. Not showing a single ounce of emotion on her face. Letting him continue. For a split second, she felt like she was listening to one of her patients.

"And why kill these kids on board the ship?" she asked.

"So you can finally see!" he barked back at her, rubbing his temples in frustration. "You still don't get it. You're just like those children. You'll never understand. You're incapable of understanding. You still choose to act irrationally. Leaving your kids to die by my hand. Cornering yourself in this room, with no way to escape me. The chaos needs to be stopped."

Butler's face contorted as if he were experiencing physical pain from the words he was speaking.

"You were so lucky to be there," he continued, his dark eyes trailing off toward the corner. "Lucky to have seen what you did. You were one of only twelve, you know. That jury. You were the witnesses to my perfection. And now, you've been blessed yet again. The sole spectator to my final act."

"I don't understand," Maria pressed, hoping to keep him talking.

"Of course you don't. You didn't understand the first time the opportunity was given to you. Even after all those weeks. Even after all the evidence. You should've seen my perfection at the trial."

Everything clicked together in Maria's mind.

That's why he's after me.

That's why he's here on this ship to begin with.

Because of how I voted as a juror.

She nodded to herself, now finally understanding Wyatt Butler in his entirety.

"You wanted to be found guilty," she said confidently.

He threw out his arms, theatrically, like Steve used to do. "I wanted to be recognized. Appreciated for the work I've done. The mastery I've shown the world. And *you* . . . you denied me of that."

A quiet moment passed between the two of them.

Maria glared at Butler with a look of defiance.

"No one appreciates what you've done, Wyatt," Maria replied through gritted teeth. "No one will ever understand. I'm going to twist and turn your story so many ways that no one ever knows the truth. Your *perfect* legacy will just be conspiracy theories and conjecture. A disheveled mess of conflicting opinions on whether you're guilty or not."

Butler's eyes widened with rage, but Maria pressed further.

"And when this is all over, Wyatt, I'll make sure *no one* will remember your name."

Butler gritted his teeth. He shook with rage.

Then he charged forward.

Straight at Maria.

41

Maria sprang to her left, dodging Butler by fractions of an inch.

His outstretched hands slammed into the diesel purifying tank.

He roared in pain.

And in that split second, she took off, sprinting toward the walkway around the corner of the railing. Massive pistons chugged on both sides. Hammering up and down with incredible force. She only had one way to go, and close behind, Butler's footsteps slapped against the concrete.

Maria raced toward the dead engineer. Leaped to the side of his prone body. The blood that had pooled around his throat had swelled to both sides of the walkway. She glanced down for a safe place to land. Somewhere to plant her foot so she wouldn't go flying.

Then something caught her eye.

The wrench.

A weapon.

Maria bent down and tugged on the metal handle jutting out of his neck. Stiff. Jammed. Caught around one of his cervical vertebrae. She yanked again, this time freeing one of the edges. More blood sprayed from the fatal wound. With one last heave, she brought the wrench up to her chest.

The handle felt damp and warm in her hand, from the blood and Butler's recent grip.

She shivered at the thought of Butler standing over the engineer, killing him for being nothing more than an inconvenience. A fly, swatted for just being in the wrong place at the wrong time. To a man like Butler, it was as simple as shelling a peanut.

Maria drew in a deep breath. Composed herself.

Butler skidded in from around the corner, knuckles raw and savage from ramming the tank. He looked ravenous. Rabid.

Maria had to be smart. She tightened her grip on the wrench. Throwing the tool was a waste of time. He could parry it away or take the hit. Better to wait for closer quarters. Until she could make a strike count.

She held her ground as he advanced. Their eyes locked. He reached within a few steps.

Maria raised the wrench over head as he dove toward her.

She slammed the titanium jaws straight into his collarbone. The metal connected with a crunching thud as she leaped to the side of the walkway.

Butler lurched past her, unable to check his momentum. He crashed to the ground and let out a deep, bellowing scream, clutching his left shoulder.

Maria spun away, preparing to run again. But the soles of her shoes slipped in the blood slick. She tried to regain full balance. Couldn't get enough traction to thrust away from him.

Butler snatched a fistful of her hair.

She wildly swung the wrench in his direction. It clanked against something solid. Maybe the rail. The impact made her lose her grip, and the tool clattered against the concrete.

Butler ripped her down, away from the wrench.

Maria screamed.

Pain shot through her scalp as her head dipped, closer and closer toward him.

Her back hit the ground. Butler jumped on top of her before she could move. She kicked her legs toward his chest, landing a hard blow to his sternum.

But it wasn't enough.

His nostrils flared. He inhaled, tasting the fear pouring off Maria's battered body. Like smelling a fine wine.

He stared down at her, sneering.

Maria attempted to punch him in the face.

Butler gripped her thrashing arms. Held her still, digging his knees into her hips, pinning her down against the cold, gritty floor. He struck her across the face with a swift backhand.

Her head whipped to the side.

A coppery taste filled Maria's mouth. Sickly and sticky. The edge of her tongue brushed past a tender tooth. Loosened from the blow.

Butler grabbed the hair above her forehead and lifted her face toward his. Maria tightened her lips and spat in his face. Flecks of blood spattered his cheeks, but he didn't flinch. In fact, he didn't even blink. Didn't wipe away the bloody saliva that was dripping down his face. Instead, he leaned in closer.

Pressing his lips up to her ear, he said, "You need to learn the consequences of your choices."

Butler wrapped his hands around Maria's throat. Squeezed her windpipe with a rigid, choking grip. Harder and harder as he peered directly into her eyes.

He slammed her head against the concrete.

Screamed into her face, "You've denied my *proof*!"

Primal and full of rage.

Butler slammed Maria's head down again. "My *legacy*!"

And again, for a painful third time. "The *perfection of my design*!"

Stars clouded the edges of Maria's vision. She felt her eyes roll back into her head. Her whole world quickly turning black. Pulses of red injected themselves through the darkness with each beat of her heart as it struggled desperately to get blood flowing to her brain.

She clawed at his face, digging her fingernails into the part of his cheeks she could reach. It had no effect. He tightened his grip. Her hands flew up to her neck. Trying desperately to pry off the stiff fingers squeezing the life out of her.

With the tiny bit of air slinking in through her trachea, she pushed out a gasping, defiant sentence . . .

"I—"

The sound came out as a wheezing croak. She felt each vibration of her crunched-up vocal cords chafing against one another.

"***I—voted—guilty.***"

Butler triumphant sneer rapidly changed to a look of confusion.

"What? No!" Butler shook his head. "*No!* You didn't!"

Maria willed more words from her injured throat.

"You *stupid* son of a bitch—" She erupted into a coughing fit. "Two years of your life wasted, going after the *wrong* juror."

Maria forced out a laugh as Butler shook his head in disbelief.

"No, no, no, you didn't!" Butler bellowed. "I saw the press conference!"

"I lied . . . you dumbass . . ." Maria grinned up at him, mustering all her remaining energy. "I covered for another juror. To protect them from all this."

Butler's face turned beet red and his eyes blinked rapidly as he continued to shake his head.

"And now," Maria pushed harder, summoning every ounce of her inner strength, "after all your hard work, after your relentless quest for perfection, all people will remember . . . is how much *you fucked all this up*."

Butler squeezed his eyes closed in anger and confusion. For an instant, his grip on Maria's neck loosened.

A final, fleeting chance she wouldn't waste. Maria thrust her leg up with a rigid jolt, burying her kneecap forcefully into Butler's groin. His hands flew from her neck and down to his lap. He let out a loud, agonizing yowl.

Maria wriggled away from his contorted body.

This was her chance . . .

Reese's head pounded as he stepped through the engine room. The gash along his hairline still dripped fresh blood into his eyes. His gun was raised. His finger on the trigger. Ready to blow away Wyatt Butler the moment the creep stepped in front of his sights.

He was close. Very close.

The sound of Butler's screams broke the consistent thrum of the engine.

Reese turned the corner along the railed walkway.

A few yards in front of him, Butler had straddled Maria, shaking her violently and throwing her head against the floor. A bloodstained wrench sat close to their side. Just beyond them, one of the crew lay dead.

Fuck.

Butler slammed Maria's head down again. "My *legacy*!"

And again. "The *perfection of my design*!"

Reese steadied his aim. The two were deadly close to one another. A misfired bullet could end Maria's life. He wiped the blood away from his brow, trying to clear his vision.

Goddamn it!

I'll hit her!

Reese's outstretched arms began to quiver. He still felt dizzy from the earlier attack. Groggy and disoriented from the head trauma. He squinted. Trying to sharpen his vision.

A gravelly, cracking voice came from the wrestling match.

Maria. Speaking too faint for Reese to understand. After a few moments, Butler's position shifted ever so slightly. Maria lifted her leg and kneed him. Hard. Butler tumbled into a pile beside her. She scurried backward on her hands, creating an inch of open space between them.

Now!

Reese pulled the trigger. The round drilled through Butler's calf. The shot reverberated around the engine room.

The right side of Butler's body collapsed. He howled in pain, but stayed upright, propping himself up on his good leg. Balancing himself with fingertips on the ground. With an excruciated wince, he hobbled toward Maria.

She took off toward Reese, sidling up beside him. She kept a hand wrapped around her throat as she gulped for air.

Reese kept his sights fixed on Butler as he collapsed back down toward the ground. The gunshot had blown a hole through the bone in his shin.

"Don't move!" Reese shouted over the engine noise.

Butler ignored him. Let out a rasping hiss. Crawled forward, leaving a trail of blood behind him, appearing desperate to continue the fight. "This won't stop, Maria!" he barked.

Reese and Maria backed farther away, stepping into the adjacent corridor. Butler charged on.

"I'll kill every single juror until I find the right one! As many as it takes before the world truly sees me!"

Reese looked to Maria. Her focus had moved off Butler. He traced her gaze up to the wall. To a bright red button and a black lever.

Butler slithered closer, dragging his shattered leg behind him like deadweight.

Reese scanned the wall until he came across a threshold's frame.

A watertight door.

He now understood the plan in her mind. Her next move confirmed it.

Maria reached up toward the lever.

Reese caught her arm just before she yanked down. "Wait—"

Maria stared down at Butler like he was a wounded animal.

She looked intent. Resolved.

Like a huntress.

Isabella.

Reese's mind flashed back to that moment in Miami over a decade ago. When he watched as the battered woman's arms crumpled down to her sides. Watched as he talked her into dropping the gun. The gun that would be turned on her just two months later. Turned on her children.

Tears brimmed alongside the blood in the corners of Reese's eyes.

He'd made this mistake once already.

He wasn't about to do it again.

Reese scanned his eyes along the upper corners of the room. Two security cameras. One pointed behind them down the corridor. The other angled back toward the taller engine mechanics.

No sights on us.

He looked down toward Maria.

Her eyes met his.

Reese blinked slowly and gave her a nod.

In an instant, Maria slammed down on the lever and slapped the button into the wall. The hydraulic center of the door hissed to life. A red alarm at the top corner of the frame sprang bright, transmitting an earsplitting ring.

Butler's eyes snapped up as he seemingly realized his mistake. He tried to wriggle backward. But his wounds wouldn't allow it. The pain in his leg likely too unbearable.

The thousand pounds of slate-colored steel crossed the walkway, creeping in on him.

He screamed. A bellowing squall. Stared up at Maria with terror in his eyes.

Reese could tell the man knew he was doomed.

The door crunched against Butler's body, crushing his chest against the frame. He shrieked. Desperate and high-pitched.

Blood spurted from his mouth.

The door continued to relentlessly close. It powered harder against him, snapping each of his ribs like frail toothpicks. His chest cavity collapsed. His lungs probably popped like balloons. The steel eventually cut through him, sending a torrent of blood and tissue up toward Maria.

She silently lurched back. Expressionless. Seemingly unmoved by the gruesome sight.

Reese peered down at Butler's severed torso. Blood spewed from his hanging entrails. Pooled up toward his lifeless head and soaked the side of his face.

Wyatt Butler's legacy.

His killing spree.

His life.

Over.

42

As she rapidly made her way back up through the decks of the ship, Maria could already imagine the newspaper headlines.

CRUISE THROUGH HELL

MURDER ON THE HIGH SEAS

KILLER IN THE CABIN NEXT DOOR

No matter which salacious titles the press would conjure up this time, the spotlight around her would be of a much different glow.

She and Reese would be hailed as heroes. A redemption story for her. The juror who'd made the mistake. Viciously attacked by the man she'd set free. Now the final purveyor of justice in a triumphant twist of fate . . .

But none of them would ever know the truth.

The truth Maria had told Butler as he choked her.

That two years ago, she really *had* voted guilty.

Maria had voted with her gut. Using her observations of Butler's attitude in the courtroom. Using her years of experience, profiling and diagnosing atypical brains. She and ten of her fellow jurors all came to the same conclusion.

But it was Ashlyn.

Sweet Ashlyn.

Unable to bring herself to condemn a man to life in prison based on merely the possibility of his guilt. Even now, after everything that'd happened, Maria never blamed her. She'd voted with her conscience. The same way Maria did.

With all the remaining strength left in her legs, Maria dashed around the corner toward the clinic, praying that the sight of two little patients inside would quell the aching throb in her chest.

Christopher came bounding out of the infirmary first. He galloped down the hallway toward Maria with open arms.

Healthy.

Safe.

Chloe followed just a few steps behind. The medical staff had done a wonderful job treating them. A few bruises and some residual grogginess from being knocked unconscious.

Nothing an IV of fluids and some rest couldn't fix. Their vitals were good and they'd both passed their concussion tests with flying colors. Each expected to make a full recovery.

Maria's bet had paid off. Without her there to witness his actions, Butler kept them alive. They became the pawns he never got to sacrifice. The pieces of his puzzle that would never fit.

Not if Maria had anything to say about it.

The twins collapsed into their mother's arms. A flood of tears and relief poured from all three. Maria tightened her hug around them. The feeling was indescribable. A kind of euphoria that eased the sting of her heartbreak.

Steve . . .

Her anchor was gone.

Trailing behind the twins, Reese and Hendricks came out of the infirmary, smiling at the sight of the family reunion.

After Hendricks had safely pulled the kids out of Butler's room, she'd stayed with them the entire night. Through their treatment at the clinic. By their bedsides when they finally woke up. Dutiful and tireless.

She made good on her promise.

And as for Reese, he had stood by and let Maria finally end all this. And for that, she'd be eternally grateful. All the families of the victims would be eternally grateful.

Maria smiled down the corridor in their direction, giving a gentle nod of gratitude to them both.

With that, she took Chloe and Christopher by their hands and turned to walk away.

As much as Maria wanted to pick up right where they'd left off, she knew her kids would be fundamentally changed after this night. Things would never really go back to the way they were. Not with the things they'd seen. The horrors they'd witnessed.

Almost as if they now shared the same pain Maria was subjected to during the trial.

It might take a decade until they were fully able to comprehend and process the torment Butler had inflicted upon them. Upon Steve. Upon their mother. She knew the road to recovery from grief and trauma was a long and winding one.

But for them, Maria had all the time in the world.

Epilogue

THREE YEARS LATER . . .

"Thank you so much, Professor Fontana."

Cameron, an especially overeager freshman in the Columbia Psychology Department, sat across from Maria in her office, nervously twiddling his thumbs against the spine of the textbook in his lap. "I overestimated the amount of time I'd have after studying for the behavioral midterm, and I only want to give you my best work. I promise you, this is a onetime thing."

Maria took a sip from a steaming coffee mug and set it back down on her desk. "It's all right, I understand. Have the essay to me by Monday and I won't deduct any points."

Cameron huffed out a sigh of relief. "Thank you. Thank you. I really appreciate it."

"Well, I appreciate you being honest with me." She extended her hand for a shake, half hoping to calm the nerves of this young man, half trying to telegraph that she wanted him to scram.

He gave her hand a sharp squeeze, stood from the armchair, and quickly shuffled out of the room. The latch on the door clacked behind him, leaving a peaceful silence in its wake.

For a moment, Maria reveled in the stillness of her office. She watched out her window as the sun set across the Van Am Quad. Groups of students wandered back to their dorms after their last classes for the week. The entire campus had that Friday glow to it.

Maria couldn't wait to get home. The twins would be getting off the bus from school any second now. The three of them had tickets to go see a movie that night, and she couldn't wait to hear about their day. Her eyes scanned across the picture on her desk.

Christopher and Chloe, now fifteen years old in the photo. Bright happy faces, arms draped around one another. Maria had to sneak her camera to the park to take that one. They'd never pose like that if they knew she was watching.

A smaller frame sat tucked behind the photo of the kids. A picture of Steve. Smiling backstage at a local production of *Fiddler on the Roof* from a few years ago. Maria always kept it close by.

To her right, an array of honors and medals stood proudly

along the edges of her desk. Following the events on board the ship three years ago, the essays she'd published on Butler's psychosis had been very well received in the psych community. And it didn't take long for the memoir she'd penned about the entire ordeal to hit number one on the *New York Times* Best Seller List. She'd even gotten a few calls from movie studios to adapt the story for the big screen.

The stack of student essays on her desk had grown twice the size since she'd returned from her last lecture. She flipped open the first cover page and gripped her red pen.

The latch on her door clicked open.

"I told you, Cameron, Monday morning is fine—"

Maria looked up through the frames of her glasses toward the door.

But it wasn't Cameron.

It was a woman. Perhaps in her late fifties. Well dressed, but with a distressed look on her face.

"Excuse me? Can I help you?" Maria asked.

"I pray you can, yes." The mysterious guest stepped into the office and quietly shut the door behind her.

"I'm sorry, ma'am, but I don't see anyone without an appointment."

For Maria, this kind of drop-in wasn't out of the ordinary. She'd occasionally had parents of students barge their way into her office before, convinced they could get their kids better grades with a little bit of bribery and some pressure. Instead, what they'd earned every time was a polite decline and a free ethics lesson from Maria.

Worse yet, this woman could be a reporter. Or one of Maria's crazed fans, still clinging to the legend of her outsmarting a serial killer after all this time.

But something about her was different. A heaviness that Maria couldn't put her finger on yet.

"Ms. Fontana, my name is Angela Grace, and I'm sorry for intruding on your private time. I'm hoping in this one instance, you'll make an exception."

"My apologies, but you'll have to call—"

"My son was murdered," she said, cutting Maria off.

The air from the room was sucked out almost instantly. Maria's look of annoyance shifted across her face. Empathy rolled in.

"He was a student. In Chicago. He was murdered. Whoever killed him did terrible things. Terrible things to him."

Maria stiffened upright in her seat. The grief poured from this woman's words and into Maria. "Ms. Grace, I am truly very sorry to hear about your loss. But I'm unsure how I can—"

"There are four others, Ms. Fontana. Four other people like my son who have been killed such as this. In the last six months."

Four others? A serial killer?

The woman's eyes teared up as she continued, "The police, the FBI haven't had any breaks in the case. They can't seem to figure the killer out, why he does what he does. How he removes bones from each victims' bodies without leaving a single incision mark. What his notes mean . . ."

"His notes?" Maria asked.

"When they found my son's body, the killer left a note that said: *KEEP CHASING SHADOWS.* Every victim gets a different note."

The killer was not just taunting the authorities. He was taunting the families. Maria could feel the cockiness behind the letter.

Keep chasing shadows . . .

Was there another, deeper meaning as well?

"My son. His name was Louis. Please. Here. I have a photo of him."

Angela dug around in the pocket of her jacket. Maria shook her head and averted her eyes.

No. Please, no.

She'd all but eliminated the horrific images from the Butler trial from her mind. To see another brutalized body might trigger them to come flooding back. Angela extended the Polaroid toward Maria. She prepared for the worst.

But through her shielded fingers, the image Maria saw was anything but grotesque.

The boy looked vibrant. In his early twenties. The same sharp bone structure as his mother's. He was handsome. Smiling on a rocky beach.

"Ms. Fontana, it's been two months since my Louis was murdered. The FBI has no leads. No one will help me." Tears openly streamed down Angela's face. Maria sat speechless. Her heart was breaking listening to her speak.

"You're the only person in the world that can help find this son of a bitch. That can figure him out and stop him before he kills again. Before he destroys another family. So, I'm begging you, Maria . . ."

Angela reached across the desk and grabbed Maria's hands.

"Will you help me?"

Acknowledgments

JAMES MURRAY

As always, I would like to thank the most charming cowriter I know, Darren Wearmouth. Not only is he a great collaborator, but he is a great friend. Even though he once got kicked out of the Caribbean Sea.

Thank you to my colleague Carsen Smith, whose incredible creativity and tireless work ethic helped bring *The Stowaway* to life.

Thanks to our excellent editor Michael Homler, our friend and colleague Steve Cohen, and the entire St. Martin's team for their incredible partnership. Thanks to my colleagues and friends Joseph, Nicole, and Ethan for their imagination and support. Thanks to Jack Rovner and Dexter Scott from Vector Management, Brandi Bowles, and our entire team from UTA, Danny Passman from GTRB, Phil Sarna and Mitch Pearlstein from PSBM, and Elena Stokes and the inventive team from Wunderkind PR. And special thanks to Brad Meltzer, R. L. Stine, James Rollins, and Steve Alten for their continued mentorship, advice, and friendship.

Mom and Dad and my entire family, I love you all. Spear and Colin—you both live to see another day . . . for now. And most importantly, thanks to my amazing wife, Melyssa, whose endless love and support makes everything worthwhile. I love you.

And finally, thanks to all the incredible *Impractical Jokers* fans around the world—you are our friends and our family!

DARREN WEARMOUTH

First, I'd like to thank my coauthor, James. He's a great guy and friend and I deeply value our partnership. Every time I visit America, James and Melyssa are always kind and generous hosts. I've missed seeing them over the past year. Second, Michael Homler, our editor from St. Martin's Press. Patience and understanding are two admirable traits among the many he possesses, and he's been a pleasure to work with. Third, my family and friends for being there. Mostly my wife and daughter, Jen and Maple, who mean the world to me. Lastly, and most importantly, a huge thanks to you for reading *The Stowaway*.